KV-202-706

Love Notes

Joanna Campbell

BANTAM BOOKS
TORONTO · NEW YORK · LONDON · SYDNEY

RL 6, IL age 11 and up

LOVE NOTES
A Bantam Book/January 1984

Cover photo by Pat Hill

ISBN 0-553-23758-6

Published simultaneously in the United States and Canada

Bantam Books are published by Bantam Books, Inc. Its trademark,
consisting of the words "Bantam Books" and the portrayal of a rooster,
is Registered in U.S. Patent and Trademark Office and in other
countries. Marca Registrada. Bantam Books, Inc., 666 Fifth Avenue,
New York, New York 10103.

Printed and bound in Great Britain by
Cox & Wyman Ltd, Reading

O   0 9 8 7 6 5 4 3 2 1

LOVE NOTES

"Mr. Caldfrey seemed happy when he listened to our duet yesterday," Kirsten said.

Peter nodded. "He told me he didn't think we needed to work on it any more, just keep it polished for the concert."

"I guess, then, we don't need to keep meeting every night." Kirsten's voice quavered unhappily.

"Kirsten—" Peter was about to speak, then changed his mind. Instead he brought his violin up to his chin and began to play. A beautiful melody filled the room, crying out with an intensity that left Kirsten stunned.

"That was beautiful," she whispered when he'd finished.

"I wrote it. Kirsten—" He set his violin down. "I wrote it for you."

Bantam Sweet Dreams Romances
Ask your bookseller for the books you have missed

Love Notes

Chapter One

The dismissal bell rang, and Kirsten Page closed her notebook, gathered her books together, and hurried from her sixth-period class to her locker. There was a worried frown on her pretty face as she made her way through the crowded hallway, avoiding a couple of near collisions with kids rushing in the opposite direction.

Wow, she thought to herself. *Peterson really laid on the homework today.* She jerked the door on her old locker open. With her music lesson after school and all that homework, when was she going to find time for her daily two hours of piano practice? she wondered. She grabbed her sweater, slammed her locker shut, and headed toward the main door. She'd have

1

to rush to get to her piano lesson on time. The buses didn't come too often.

"Hey, Kirsten!" It was Barbara Santi, a girl she had gotten to know that year because they were in several classes together.

Barbara caught up with her, and together they walked to the door. "Listen, some of the girls are coming over to my house tomorrow after school. We want to get our outfits together for the junior country-and-western dance. Want to come?"

"I'd love to! Oh, no." Kirsten's face fell. "I can't. I have to baby-sit late tomorrow afternoon, and before that I have to do some practicing."

"Can't you put off the practicing until another day?"

"I wish I could, but I've already lost a couple of hours this week."

"Boy, I'd die if I had your schedule! You never have any free time!"

"I know. I really don't like it this way, but what can I do?"

"But you're going to the junior dance, aren't you?"

"I'll try. I'd really like to."

"I'd do more than try if I were you. Richie Mayer will be there. I see the way he looks at you all the time in history class."

Kirsten had noticed, too, and she was pretty

flattered. Richie was on the football team, which meant he was very popular, and he was tall, dark, and gorgeous. Yet Kirsten knew the only time they ever talked was when Richie asked to borrow her history notes. "He's just a friend, sort of."

Barbara's eyes widened. "Well, friend or not, *I* certainly wouldn't mind having him look in *my* direction! And he might be more interested if you showed up at some of the dances and stuff, or some of the football games. Believe me, I know guys, and you've got to go out of your way to show a little interest in the things they like."

"I guess—it's just that I don't have time." Kirsten glanced at her watch. "Darn, I've got to go, Barbara, or I'll be late. Thanks for asking me tomorrow. I really wish I could come."

"Yeah. Well, maybe some other time."

Kirsten could already see the enthusiasm in Barbara's eyes fading. *She thinks I'm a nerd*, Kirsten thought to herself.

"See ya."

"Yeah, see ya, Barbara."

As Kirsten sprinted through the open door, she wondered if it was all worth it—this dream of hers to be a concert pianist. There was so much work and sacrifice involved. It wasn't the work she minded, though. She loved the piano, and practicing was actually a pleasure. But squeezing in everything else was the tough part. She couldn't let her grades slip if she wanted to get into a really good music school, and she couldn't stop baby-sitting because she needed the money. With four kids in her family, the least she could do was help pay for her music lessons. In the end she never had any free time for herself.

Her schedule really hadn't bothered her all that much until that year: it was her junior year, and the girls she knew were always running off on dates or to basketball games, club meetings, or parties. It seemed that whenever she was asked to join them, she had to say no. After a while she knew they'd stop asking. It wasn't meanness. They'd just forget about her and go their own ways with other kids who had time to do what they wanted to do. The same thing happened with boys. With her gently waving, long black hair, long, dark lashes and blue eyes, Kirsten should have been flooded with dates, but word had gotten around about her schedule and involvement in the piano. Since most of the kids thought classical music was boring, boys rarely asked her out, figuring she was weird because she played that kind of music.

It's not fair, she thought, clutching her books more tightly under her arm as she saw the bus coming up the hill. *But what am I going to do about it?* She really felt left out.

With the fare ready in her free hand, Kirsten boarded the bus that would take her to her piano teacher's house. She both liked and respected Mr. Jennings. He'd been a concert pianist, having even played with the New York Philharmonic, but now he was retired and taught gifted students in Fairly, Connecticut. Four years before, Kirsten's previous teacher had set up an audition for her with Jennings. He had accepted her as a student, and over the years they had developed a close relationship. Jennings was strict but encouraging: Kirsten couldn't believe how much she'd improved studying with him. Suddenly she was angry with herself. *Why am I so down about missing Barbara's get-together? I'm lucky—luckier than most of the kids. I've got a great teacher and my music.* But underneath it all, Kirsten was lonely.

The bus dropped her at the corner. Kirsten walked the two blocks to Mr. Jennings's cheery yellow house, letting herself in through the door that opened into the studio. The room was bright and sunny. Mr. Jennings sat at his desk in one corner, his steel gray head bent over a pile of papers. He looked up and smiled.

"Well, right on time, Kirsten. I could set my watch by you. Why don't you run through a few

5

Czerny exercises while I finish this work? It won't take me long."

Kirsten sorted through her books and found her music, took off her jacket, and went to the grand piano in the center of the room.

She'd run through several exercises before she sensed Mr. Jennings behind her.

"Staccato," he commented. "Keep the touch light but sharp. Good."

After a few minutes he stopped her. "Let's go on to your lesson pieces. You were working on a Scarlatti sonata, the Mozart piece—" He frowned. "And a third."

"The Chopin Prelude in D Minor."

"Ah yes, how could I forget. Begin with that. The arpeggios are a real test of skill."

Kirsten had chosen this piece herself, and she'd practiced it enthusiastically at home, but now her mind wasn't fully on what she was doing. Several times Mr. Jennings told her to stop, go back a few measures, and begin again.

"No, Kirsten," he broke in. "That passage should be allegro appassionato! Bum-ba-bum—" He began clapping his hands together. "Not so slowly. Again—brightly, with feeling."

When he was finally satisfied, he told her to begin the Mozart. Kirsten had been working on the piece for weeks, but she realized as she watched her fingers moving mechanically from one note to the next that she had no feeling for it. She was playing without expression, putting no life into the music. When she took her fingers from the keys, Mr. Jennings sat down beside her on the piano bench.

"Something is on your mind, Kirsten, isn't it? You're performing like a wooden soldier. Anything you can talk to me about?"

Kirsten dropped her eyes, gripping her hands in her lap. How could she explain her confusion to Mr. Jennings? Why was she suddenly so dissatisfied with her goals? After all he'd done for her, could she even mention it to him? Would he understand? At last, because she had to talk to someone about her feelings, she began hesitantly.

"I'm really sorry, Mr. Jennings. It's just that the last couple of weeks—today especially—I feel like all I ever do is work—the piano, homework, baby-sitting! There's never any time to have fun or go out on dates or just hang out with the girls. They're all having such good times. I feel like I'm missing out."

Mr. Jennings looked at Kirsten's profile; she was frowning. "What you're feeling is very normal. I remember my own daughter when she was about your age. She's a professional and doing very well with her music now, and I'm extremely proud of her. But there was a time when she began to lose interest. She felt confused and was certain life was passing her by because she was playing her violin while her friends were out enjoying themselves. And, of course, very few of them shared her interest in serious music. She couldn't pull out her violin and play a bit of Stravinsky and expect her friends to be entertained."

"And?"

"At first I didn't understand. I was impatient. But then I thought back to some of my rough periods. So I tried understanding and talking. I told my daughter to think ahead to what she might feel in three or four years if she gave up her music. Once the novelty of all the fun had worn off, wouldn't she look back with regret? At sixteen it might seem that the good times are passing you by, but they won't—that I promise you. There's nothing wrong with wanting to be with your friends. Everyone needs friendship, but you should try to find a happy medium.'"

"That's just it, Mr. Jennings. I have no time. And now I'm beginning to think I haven't got the dedication it takes to become a concert pianist."

"Nonsense! Don't let me hear you talk like that. We all have times when our enthusiasm and motivation start to give out—it's natural. No matter how dedicated we are, we all need encouragement occasionally to get back on the right track. At the moment you're going through one of those uncertain periods. It will pass."

"Do you think so?"

"I'm sure of it. If you have any doubts, think of what you've accomplished so far. And then think of how far we both know you can go. Have you tried talking to your parents about your feelings?"

"No. I was afraid they'd be disappointed if I expressed any doubts."

"They're very proud of your talent and what you've done with it, but it's your future, and *you* have to decide what you want. But *I* think you owe it to yourself not to throw it all away."

Kirsten thought of the dream she'd had of sitting on a concert stage, her fingers bringing beautiful music to life. She thought of the hours of work she'd put in to accomplish her dream, the sacrifices she'd made, the pride in her parents' eyes when they listened to her play—and her own satisfaction and pride, which was the most important part.

"You're right, Mr. Jennings." She sighed. "I haven't been thinking very straight."

"No, you've been thinking straight, and your problem is a difficult one. But all I'm saying is that for now continue with the piano and your dream of a concert career. Maybe later you will give it up. I hope not."

Kirsten grinned.

"And what harm would there be in taking some time off once in a while to be with your friends? Why don't you take a night off?"

"The junior dance," Kirsten said, almost to herself.

"There, you see. Your parents aren't going to begrudge you a little fun. They don't strike me as heartless people."

"They're not. They're the best, and they've never tried to force me into music. It's always been my own decision."

"And think of all you have to look forward to. There's a good chance you'll get into the Trilling Conservatory of Music after you graduate next year, and in a few weeks you'll be going up to Greenacres to perform with the student orchestra for the summer. Now that's really a feather in your cap. They accept only the best."

Kirsten knew that the opportunity to study at Greenacres, the beautiful former estate in northwestern Connecticut, was fantastic. Some major symphonies played summer concerts there as did many of the finest soloists. The student program was one of the best around. She was excited, but nervous, too. Was she really asking too much to have a great social life and all this, too?

"I'm sorry, Mr. Jennings," she said finally. "I know you're right. I just get down sometimes."

"Only natural."

"I *am* looking forward to this summer, and I'm—I'm sorry I bothered you with all of this, Mr. Jennings, but thanks for talking to me."

"It was my pleasure, Kirsten. I've heard that's what teachers are for. Now let's run through the Mozart again. I think we'll both hear an improvement."

"You bet."

Chapter Two

During the last month of the school year, Kirsten recaptured her enthusiasm for the piano. Mr. Jennings had been right—her dream was too important to throw away. Even her homework was no longer such a chore now that she had her dedication back.

Since Kirsten's father was away on a business trip and had the family car, Mr. Jennings volunteered to drive Kirsten to Greenacres four Sundays later. Kirsten had been to concerts on the famous grounds, but Mr. Jennings was personally acquainted with the layout of the former estate, so he could help her get settled. He even knew some staff members.

As they drove north, Kirsten thought back

over her last weeks at school. She especially remembered the junior dance, for which she'd had such high expectations. She'd gone with Barbara and some of the other girls, and she'd spent hours in her room getting ready. She'd borrowed her brother's cowboy hat and a vest, as well as a pair of Barbara's boots; she'd even spent part of her baby-sitting money on a new checked western shirt.

Richie had asked her to dance. At first she'd been in heaven. He was so good-looking, and all the other girls seemed a bit envious of her as she'd walked to the dance floor with him. For a minute she'd felt like a queen. But then they'd tried to talk. As Barbara had advised, she'd asked him about his interest—football. But she'd never had the time to go to the games, so she didn't know a whole lot about the game. She became bored, and almost immediately the conversation petered out. Then he brought up music.

"You know music. You must like the new Journey album."

"I haven't heard it."

He looked surprised. "You've heard some of the cuts, though."

"I don't think so."

"Geez! Where have you been? I thought you played the piano."

"I do, but I study classical."

"Oh, that stuff. Some of it's OK, I guess. My folks listen to it. You'll have to come over to my place sometime this summer and listen to some of my albums."

Kirsten sighed. *Here we go again,* she thought. "I'd love to, but I won't be here."

"Oh? Where you going?"

"To Greenacres in northern Connecticut for their summer music program."

"Never heard of it."

"It's a great place. They give outdoor performances. A lot of famous symphony orchestras play there."

"You looking forward to that?" His expression told her that he thought she was pretty bizarre if she was.

"Oh, yes. It's a chance at something really special."

He hadn't much to say for the rest of their dance. And when the song had ended, he led her to the side. The look of interest that had been in his eyes when he'd asked her to dance was gone.

"Well, catch you later, Kirsten. Maybe in history class."

Richie hadn't gone near her for the rest of the night. She went home feeling more left out than ever.

Kirsten brought her mind back to the present as Mr. Jennings made some comment on the scenery as they drove along. She was feeling better about herself; she had something terrific to look forward to. She would forget the bad times in Fairly—the guys who thought she was out of it, and the girls she could never spend time with.

Finally they entered the long drive leading to the main grounds of Greenacres. Sensing her nervousness, Mr. Jennings laid his hand over hers briefly.

"Nothing to worry about, dear. You'll find everyone friendly—a very nice group of kids. And I'll stay around awhile to see you settled in. I did promise your mother."

Kirsten smiled and remembered her mother's teary goodbye. "I'll be all right, and I'll have to get used to meeting new people. I'll be going away to school after next year."

"Well, here we are." Jennings pulled the car into the parking lot near the entrance to a large building, which had once been the main house on the estate.

"You'll register here," he said as he checked his watch. "But we have time. Why don't we take a walk around the grounds? Couldn't be a more beautiful day." There wasn't a cloud in the light blue sky; the sunlight shone on the thick green lawns. Miles of rolling hills glistened in the distance.

"Let's start with the outdoor stage, and then we can circle back here to get you registered." Mr. Jennings headed down one of the brick paths, Kirsten walking briskly at his side.

They stopped in front of a large covered stage, its semicircular front open to the lawns surrounding it. Kirsten remembered several summer Sundays sitting on a blanket with her parents under the shade of one of the spreading trees, happily listening to performances of Beethoven, Haydn, Mozart, and Tchaikovsky.

"It's quiet today," Jennings commented, "but wait until next weekend when the season starts." He smiled to himself. "And wait until the day you sit under that roof and perform."

The thought sent butterflies to Kirsten's stomach, but she was happy in addition to being scared.

They walked through the gardens. Snuggled behind them were various small cottages, which Mr. Jennings said were rehearsal sheds. Soon they were back in front of the main building, looking out to the hills and the distant shimmering lake.

"Tour over," said Jennings. "I think it's time we got you registered, then I'll take you to your dorm and get your luggage unloaded."

Registration went quickly, and Mr. Jennings spoke to a few people he knew. Kirsten was assigned a room in a building at the far side of the grounds.

They drove over to the dorm and were greeted by a smiling middle-aged woman.

"Hello. I'm Mrs. Vertel. Can I help you?"

"Yes, I'm Kirsten Page. I'm supposed to be rooming here."

"William Jennings." He extended his hand.

Mrs. Vertel accepted it. "How do you do. Kirsten, your room's right up this way—you'll be sharing it with two other girls. Why don't you follow me."

She led them up a flight of stairs and down a short hall to a door on the right. She knocked softly, and someone answered, "Come in."

Two girls about Kirsten's age were in the midst of unpacking their bags. A cello stood in a corner, a violin case on one of the beds.

"Girls, your third roommate," Mrs. Vertel said cheerfully. "This is Kirsten Page. Kirsten, Rene Schulman." She indicated the taller, auburn-haired girl.

"Nice to meet you, Kirsten."

"And Sharlie Watson." The petite blond gave Kirsten a shy smile.

"I'll let you get to know each other," Mrs.

Vertel said. "I imagine when you registered they gave you a schedule, maps, and whatnot."

"Yes."

"Good. Then, as you know, the rest of the day is yours to do as you please; we'll have a buffet dinner ready downstairs in the dining room at six. Breakfast and dinner are served here; lunch is served picnic-style, right by the rehearsal hall." She turned toward the door. "Oh, and if you need anything, just let me know. You'll find me in the office to the side of the front hall until eight or so. Enjoy yourselves."

"Well," Mr. Jennings said, "I guess I'll be on my way, too—unless you'd like me to stay a bit longer."

"Oh, no. I'm fine. You've done so much already. I can't tell you how much I appreciate every-thing." Kirsten noticed that Mr. Jennings was still holding the larger of her suitcases, and she looked quickly around the room.

Rene interpreted the look. "We left you the bed over there by the windows, if that's OK."

"Oh, sure. I can look out at the view."

Mr. Jennings stepped over to the bed and hoisted the suitcase onto it.

"Kirsten, I wish you luck," he said quietly. "Though I know you don't need it. You'll do beautifully. And I'll be in touch," he added, grinning, "just to get an occasional progress report. Of course, I want you to call me if you have any problems or questions. You have your music?"

She laughed. "It was the first thing I packed. All safe and sound right in here." She patted the suitcase.

"Good. Now work hard but have some fun, too." He smiled and walked to the door. "Very nice to meet you, girls."

Kirsten reached up and gave Mr. Jennings a kiss on the cheek, which immediately caused the dignified man to blush.

"Thanks again, Mr. Jennings."

"I'm sure you'll make me proud, Kirsten."

"I'm going to try, Mr. Jennings."

There was a moment of self-conscious silence after Mr. Jennings left, then Rene grinned.

"Your music teacher, I'll bet."

"How'd you guess?"

"Mine said the same things, though she didn't bring me up here. What do you play?"

"Piano."

"Violin," said Rene.

"Cello," Sharlie added.

"Let's hurry up and get unpacked," Rene urged. "Then we can take a walk. I want to do some exploring."

The three girls began filling dresser drawers

and closets and arranging books and music on the shelves.

"Where are you from?" Rene asked in a friendly voice.

"Fairly, Connecticut. How about you?"

"New Jersey, Harrington, and Sharlie's from Pennsylvania. You didn't have a very long drive up here then."

"No. A little over two hours."

"Have you ever been up here before?"

"A couple of times for concerts."

"I hadn't. I'd seen pictures, but I didn't expect it to be so pretty." Rene paused as she straightened a blouse on a hanger. "Have you met any of the other kids yet?"

"Just you two." Kirsten paused, then admitted, "I was a little nervous coming up here when I didn't know anyone. And I was terrified they'd put me in with college kids. You're not, are you?"

At that Sharlie looked up. "No, we're high school seniors, too. "Boy, does it make me feel good to hear you say you were nervous, too. I've always been so shy. I was petrified—nearly backed out. But Rene's been so friendly, I feel much better."

Rene laughed. "Yeah, shyness has never been one of my weaknesses. People usually tell me I have the opposite problem—I don't know how to keep my mouth shut. But I'm really looking forward to this summer, just to be with kids who like what I like. I always feel like a real weirdo at home. You two ever get that? You know, you tell kids in school you're into classical music, and they look at you like you're a nut or something?"

"All the time." Sharlie sighed. "Of course, I was never very popular anyway, so I've always been glad I've had my music."

"But you're so cute!" Rene exclaimed.

Sharlie giggled shyly. "And so quiet I fade into the background. I don't know how to talk to people, and when I'm in a crowd, I sort of end up hiding out in a corner."

"Well, we'll soon fix that," said Rene firmly. "Don't look upset. I love to solve people's problems."

"Please, Rene, don't. Being pushed only makes me worse."

"Don't worry. I'd never push. Hey, do you guys know that the majority of kids here are in college—that means *college guys.* Hope they're looking for high-school seniors, who are cute, witty, talented, and very shy and modest." Her mood was contagious, and pretty soon both Kirsten and Sharlie were laughing. "We ready for that walk?"

21

"I am," Kirsten replied, closing her case. "I can put away the rest of my stuff later."

"Me, too." Sharlie had brightened up. "I didn't get to see much of anything when we registered."

As the three left the building, Kirsten whispered to Sharlie, "I know what you mean about dating. I don't exactly have the guys waiting in line either."

As the girls ambled along the beautiful, broad lawns, Kirsten asked, "What got you two started in music? You said you play the cello, Sharlie?"

"Mmm. My family was always musical. My father's a musician. He started me out playing, and I just fell in love with it."

"What about you, Rene?"

"Well, no one ever dreamed I had any special musical talent. My parents thought it would be a good idea if I tried out the violin through the elementary school program. It went along with the tennis and ballet lessons—you know, so I was well-rounded and all that. I surprised them all, including myself, by loving the violin. It just came so naturally, not like sweating and struggling on a hot tennis court. Now my ambition is to be first violinist with the New York Philharmonic if it kills me, and it probably will. I may be eighty before I get there!"

"I have a dream like that, too," Kirsten confided. "Sitting up on a concert stage playing

Chopin or Rachmaninoff—what a feeling it must be."

"Where are you thinking of going after high school?"

"I'm hoping to get accepted to Trilling in New York," Kirsten said.

"That's just about the best, but some of the liberal arts colleges have good music programs, too. I'm applying to a couple. What about you, Sharlie?"

"Mid-Western State. Madeline Partrell teaches there, and she's one of the best cello teachers around."

"Yeah. I have one of her recordings."

"Well, we'll be working with the best this summer, too," Kirsten commented, "to give us a little taste of the big time."

They all laughed.

Kirsten smiled to herself. It was going to be a good summer. Already she'd met two great girls who shared her deepest interest. It was so fantastic finding people her own age who thought and felt like she did. Already she felt perfectly at home.

Chapter Three

The next morning Kirsten reached groggily for the screaming alarm clock; the confusion of not finding it in its normal place roused her. She sat up quickly in bed, stared around her, then finally realized she was at Greenacres, not in her familiar bedroom. The alarm wasn't hers after all but Rene's.

Sharlie was awake, too, but Rene slept on, dead to the world, her pillow over her head.

"I don't believe her," Kirsten mumbled, sliding from between the sheets and stumbling over to press the alarm button. "Whew. That's better."

"Wake her up," Sharlie said. "Why should we be the only ones to suffer."

"You're right." Kirsten grabbed the covers and pulled them back ruthlessly. When that produced no effect, she grabbed the pillow, dropped it on the floor, and lowered her mouth to near Rene's ear. "Come on, Rene. Time to get up!"

"Huh! What're you doing!" Rene jumped. "Let me alone! I want to sleep." She reached blindly for the covers that were no longer there.

"Time to get up," Kirsten repeated insistently. Sharlie was laughing from her bed. Finally, a little bit of feet tickling got Rene up.

"Oh," she said, moaning. "I think I'm dead."

"You always like this in the morning?" Sharlie asked.

"I should have warned you. My single vice is that I'm terrible to wake up. Oh, and today's such a big day."

"I'll say. We have to be at the rehearsal hall in an hour, so we'd better hurry."

After a quick breakfast downstairs, where they had a chance to meet some of the other girls in their dorm, they set off across the grounds: Rene and Sharlie with instruments in hand and Kirsten with a folder of music. A number of other kids, all carrying instruments, were walking in the same direction. It seemed a longer walk than it had the afternoon before, especially for Sharlie, who was lugging her cello.

"Want me to take it for you for a while?" Kirsten asked.

"No, I'm used to it—goes with the instrument."

"Yeah," Rene said, laughing. "My music teacher wanted me to try the cello for variety, and that's the main reason I wouldn't. But let one of us help you. You'll be worn out before we get to rehearsal."

"Well, OK, but just for a minute."

Kirsten took the cello since Rene already had her violin.

"And I'll take your music," Sharlie offered, then laughed, "it's what I'd call an unfair swap."

The rehearsal hall sat in the far corner of the grounds. From the outside it looked like a barn misplaced on the elegant Greenacres lawn. But inside it was more like a concert hall. The large, high-ceilinged main room was outfitted with a stage with platforms; there were benches in the audience. Modern lighting in the roof above the stage supplemented the natural daylight that filtered in through skylights.

The hall was in confusion as students wandered in through each of the three doors, not knowing exactly what to do or where to go. The girls went to the stage and found their own sections, taking any of the chairs until there were definite seat assignments. For Kirsten it was easy. There was only one grand piano, and it stood on the left side of the stage.

After about fifteen minutes, when most of the students had found their sections, a short, stocky, balding man walked briskly down the center aisle and up the steps to the podium. Immediately the noisy chatter in the room began to subside, although some whispering was still heard under the scraping of chairs and the rattling of music stands.

The man rapped his baton on the conductor's podium. "Boys and girls, let's settle down." A hush. "For the moment why don't you take the chair closest to you so you'll be comfortable while I make my little speech."

More shuffles as a few kids looked around them and found chairs. One boy who was left without a seat slipped noisily out of one row, stumbling over legs and instrument cases, and into the next row.

"First, let me introduce myself. My name is Gerald Caldfrey, conductor for the ensemble orchestra during your stay here. There will be guest conductors coming in from time to time, and of course, a celebrity conductor for your last performance. I will withhold his or her identity for the time being for fear of diminishing my own importance."

There were chuckles from the orchestra, then

Mr. Caldfrey continued. "During the course of our study, we will break up into quartets and chamber music groups, with solos and duets here and there. The idea is to give you a well-rounded perspective of the music world and also to help you build your individual talents through working and coordinating with others, and, need I say, letting you all have exposure to some of the best professionals in the field.

"As you in the string and wind sections know, first and second seats were determined by your auditions. These can change over the course of the summer, however, so I want no one to get cocky, nor others to lose hope. Now, let's introduce ourselves. I'd like each of you to stand in turn and tell us your name. After all, if we can't work well together as a group, we can't hope to get our music across to our audience. Let's begin with the back row wind and percussion section." Mr. Caldfrey pointed to the boy on the left end of the last row.

Kirsten looked up over her shoulder. The poor pimply-faced boy who had to start roll call looked as if he'd like to slide into his shoes.

Kirsten didn't pay particular attention until a tall, blond boy in the first violinist's seat stood up. He seemed to stand out from the others—not just for his looks, which were coolly handsome, but his air. He had total assurance; he seemed to know just where he was and what he wanted. He stood up boldly, his violin under his arm, and looked directly at Mr. Caldfrey. "I'm Peter Restrochek."

He sat down, but Kirsten's eyes remained on him. She almost missed Rene rising to announce herself. Kirsten was last. As she rose from the piano bench, she saw the tall blond's eyes on her, studying her, but there was no smile on his lips. "Kirsten Page," she said quietly.

"Well," Mr. Caldfrey said, "now that we all know each other, shall we begin this rehearsal? As for seating, if you are in your own section, remain where you are. I'll call off the first and second chairs, and you can arrange yourselves appropriately."

Kirsten let her mind wander until he called out, "First violinist, Peter Restrochek. Second violinist, Rene Schulman."

Good for Rene, Kirsten thought. But what particularly interested Kirsten was that Peter Restrochek remained in the first.

After they had shuffled themselves around, Mr. Caldfrey raised his hands for silence. "Let's begin. I believe you all have the scores for Schubert's Symphony no. 4 in C minor—the *Tragic*. Get your music in order. Need I say I presume you have all rehearsed before you arrived here."

He lifted his baton. The orchestra was immediately poised. Then, on the downbeat, they began. It was only the first rehearsal, but still the music sounded beautiful to Kirsten. When the strings came in, she listened carefully, first concentrating on Rene and Sharlie, then her eyes and ears focused on the first violinist. She knew, just by watching the sweep of his bow and listening to his leads to the others in the violin section, that he could someday be a master. He played with such emotion and freedom!

Mr. Caldfrey led them all the way through the piece, then dropped his baton on his stand. "For a first run-through I shouldn't complain— but percussionists, you came in too fast in the third movement; woodwinds, you missed your forte; horns, you were off tempo and a measure too late; cellos, you, too, but I shouldn't blame you, you were only following the horns. Again, my musical friends! And this time, be more precise!"

The next run-through went well, even better than Mr. Caldfrey expected, judging from the expression on his face. He led them through the next orchestra piece.

It was in this number that Kirsten had to

play a piano solo with a solo violin. Mr. Caldfrey pointed to her, and she began the overture. Yet, for all her nervousness, her fingers were hitting the right keys—but was the expression there? Mr. Caldfrey motioned with his baton toward the first violin. Peter Restrochek came in with a soulful melody line, full of pain and anguish. Kirsten came back with a lighter answer. Then the full orchestra entered sympathetically.

By the time they'd run through the piece once, everyone was ready for lunch. Kirsten continued to sit at the piano, analyzing her performance, until Rene and Sharlie ran over to her.

"It was great, don't you think?" Rene burst out. "We sound almost professional!"

"I had the best time." Sharlie smiled, her face bright.

"It was good—I mean considering we're beginners," Kirsten said. "But I know he's going to come back with lots of criticisms."

"Of course he will. That's part of why it's fun," Rene stated. "But still it sounded pretty good."

The girls went outside, stood in line to get sandwiches and drinks from the picnic table set up nearby, then sat under a tree to eat.

"You did really well on that overture," Rene told Kirsten.

"Thanks. I was a nervous wreck."

"I sure would have been."

"The guy who's first violinist seemed pretty cool about it all," Sharlie mused as she took a bite of her sandwich.

"He's something, isn't he?" Rene said. "I talked to him a little when we switched music. He's not very friendly, though—nice enough when I asked him a question about the score, but strictly business. And, boy, can he play! I thought I was pretty good, but watching and listening to him brought me down to earth real quick."

"Maybe he's just shy," Sharlie suggested.

"He's so talented," Kirsten said.

"Not bad to look at either, though myself, I've never been partial to blonds—give me a tall, dark, and handsome guy anytime." Rene laughed. "Actually give me any guy at all who shows some interest, and I'd be satisfied."

"You're a nut, Rene," Kirsten said, grinning. She thought about Peter and how he had stared at her during the introductions. "I wonder where he's from," she mused.

"I'll ask around and see if I can find out anything else about the mysterious Mr. Restrochek," Rene said.

"Why don't you just ask him?"

"He might say it's none of my business."

"That doesn't sound like something that would stop you."

"I'm not *that* bad, Kirsten. Occasionally I know when to keep my mouth shut. He's different," Rene said, suddenly serious. "I feel like I'd be a little shy with him myself."

"That must be some kind of a record!"

For a moment Rene looked hurt. "Do you guys really think I'm that pushy?"

"Oh, no, of course not," Kirsten answered. "We're just teasing you. Anyway, you're the one who told us you're never shy—we hardly know you. Hey, finish eating. We've got to go soon. We don't want to be late on the first day."

The afternoon rehearsal went even better than the morning session. Everyone seemed up, and even Mr. Caldfrey looked pleased. At three o'clock he put down his baton.

"Shall we call it an afternoon? I'll be meeting with all of you individually to work out your programs. Tomorrow morning I'd like the string section to meet with me here at nine. At ten the woodwinds and brass, and at eleven the percussionists. There'll be rehearsal for the entire orchestra immediately after lunch. Everything clear?"

There was a mumble of assent from the students.

"Good. Then have a pleasant afternoon, and if I could see our pianist and first violinist at the side of the stage now."

Kirsten was startled by the request. *Was there something wrong with their playing?* she wondered as she hurried over to Mr. Caldfrey's podium. Peter Restrochek joined them.

Mr. Caldfrey smiled. "I wanted to speak to you for a moment about the piano and violin solos we rehearsed today. I thought you both did very well, but I believe that section will need a little additional work. Do you know each other?"

"Only from introductions this morning," Kirsten said, glancing over at Peter. He was looking at her intently, his blue eyes serious but aloof.

She extended her hand. "Kirsten Page. Nice to meet you."

Peter clasped her hand firmly. "You, too. Peter Restrochek."

Kirsten liked the sound of his voice, yet she felt uncomfortable under his steady gaze. She smiled a little nervously.

Mr. Caldfrey continued. "What I had in mind was the two of you practicing the solo section together—perhaps this afternoon and an hour or two each day when you can fit it into your schedules. Let's have a look at the score. There are a few things I want to point out."

The hall was quiet now, for the last of the

students had left. Mr. Caldfrey flipped through his sheets of music until he found the passage in question. "Right here, Peter, where we go into the con forte, you'll need to bring out the melody line more strongly while Kirsten will be playing pianissimo. And here, you need to work on the timing a bit. . . ."

Both Kirsten and Peter listened closely as he continued. His suggestions were justified and well made. When he'd finished, Mr. Caldfrey glanced up at them. "Any questions?"

"Not at the moment," Peter said thoughtfully.

"Then suppose I show you the rehearsal room." He moved away from the podium. "There's a room here in this building behind the stage. As you probably know, there are a number of rehearsal studios scattered around the grounds, but not all of them have pianos."

He led them down a side hallway, stopping before a door. "I believe this room's free." He swung the door inward. "Come on in."

Kirsten glanced quickly around the small room. A weathered baby grand took up a good portion of the floor space. A few folding chairs and music stands were shoved into one corner.

"You should find everything you need here."

Peter immediately walked toward one of the music stands and repositioned it.

"If you don't have any other questions," Mr. Caldfrey said, "I'll leave you on your own. Should you need me, my office is a few doors down, and I'd be more than happy to help if I can. Otherwise, I'll see you both tomorrow."

Chapter Four

After Mr. Caldfrey left the room, Kirsten moved uneasily toward the piano. She wondered if Peter felt the same discomfort and awkwardness she did. He certainly didn't seem to as he unsnapped his violin case and sorted through his music. She arranged her own music on the piano and glanced surreptitiously at Peter as he carefully retuned his instrument. How handsome he was, she thought, with his thick blond hair and even features. Yet he was so reserved, so serious—so different from the boys at school. He was intriguing. *What's he like underneath?* she wondered.

"Are you ready? How about if we run through it once, then work on the weak parts?"

The sound of his voice surprised her, and she looked down self-consciously. "Sure. That sounds like a good idea." She shifted the piano bench into position, then began the overture. As the music built and Peter joined in, Kirsten soon lost all nervousness, forgetting everything but the beautiful sounds they were creating. Hearing Peter play for the first time without the orchestra in the background, Kirsten was doubly awed by his talent and the feeling he put into the music. A lot of musicians could have played each note correctly, but only the most gifted could get to the soul of the music the way he did.

When the last note had died away, Kirsten took her fingers from the keys and looked up at Peter. "That was fantastic!"

He seemed surprised and glanced at her sharply. "We need a lot more work. The transition passages aren't blending smoothly enough."

"Oh, I know that. I was talking about your melody lead—it was perfect."

For a moment he was flustered by her praise. He looked away. "I've always liked this piece."

"So have I. Though I've never played it before for full orchestra—only as arranged for piano. The violin brings out so much more." She hesitated, fingering her music. "Where are you from, Peter? Is this your first summer at Green-acres?"

He nodded to the last question. "I'm from New Jersey."

"Oh, really? So is Rene, the second violinist. She's one of my roommates."

"She told me at rehearsal. She's from a very different part. I'm from Newark. I've been study-ing at Trilling in New York City the last year," he added, "so I haven't been home much."

"How do you like Trilling? That's where I'm applying."

"It's what I've always wanted. I'm studying under Theodore Mendal, who's really helping me with what I want to achieve."

"Which is?"

"A solo concert tour. I'm looking forward to going to Chicago for the Young Soloists Con-cert Series with Mendal next year. It's a real honor to be chosen. I should get some recogni-tion out of it."

Kirsten studied him. He was looking away from her now, nervously playing with his music. He was really reaching for the top, she mused, but he just might have the talent to do it. "Do you find it a lot of work at Trilling?"

"My music isn't work. It's all I've ever wanted."

"I can understand that. I feel the same. You started playing young?"

"Six. One of our neighbors in our apartment building played. He was an old man who'd never had any professional training—played strictly by ear. But he saw my interest and started to teach me. He even loaned me his violin to practice. When I was ten, I got a paper route and ran errands for money. That's when I started professional lessons. My parents didn't have the extra money, and besides which, they thought my lessons were an extravagance. The old man and I used to play together all the time. He died two years ago."

"I'm sorry. He sounds like he was a real friend."

At last he smiled briefly, caught up in a memory. "He was—always told me I could reach whatever I wanted if I worked for it hard enough."

"Hearing you today, I know you can. Good luck, though. It's a hard path."

"Thanks." Then he immediately became more businesslike. "We'd better get back to work."

They practiced without stopping for another forty minutes, going through rough sections again and again. He was a perfectionist, Kirsten was discovering, but she tended to be one herself when it came to her music.

She felt emotionally drained but satisfied when they'd finished running through the piece one last time. They'd accomplished a lot, and they were sounding good together. Peter seemed pleased, too, more relaxed and friendly than at first.

As he carefully returned his violin to its case, he asked quietly, "And what about you? I mean where are you from?" He didn't look at her as he spoke.

"I'm from Connecticut, a town called Fairly. I don't know if you've heard of it."

"I drove through there once with a guy from Trilling. Seemed like a nice town—a lot different from where I grew up. How'd you get into music?"

"It's the old story, I've loved the piano since I was big enough to sit on the bench. We had an old upright that had been my grandmother's, and when I started taking lessons, I just knew someday I wanted to sit on a concert stage. It's seemed impossible sometimes, but I guess I'm almost there. One more year of high school, then Trilling, I hope. Then I'll see if I can make it in the professional world."

"You're going to make a career of the piano?" From the tone of his voice, he sounded almost surprised. Kirsten figured she'd imagined it, though. Why should he think her ambition was strange when he wanted the same thing?

"I'd like to, if I'm good enough. Of course, I'll know that better when I get to college and see what kind of competition I'm up against."

He nodded and finally looked over at her. "We need more practice," he said in his most businesslike voice. "My schedule's going to be pretty full, what with master classes and section rehearsals, and I want to go to as many concerts as possible."

"Me, too. We could always get together and practice after dinner. On the nights of concerts, we could rehearse for an hour or so before the concert. OK?"

He was silent for a moment, then nodded. "I can meet you here tomorrow night at seven."

He stood with his case in his hand while Kirsten rose from the piano bench and gathered up her music. He awkwardly held the door for her as they stepped out of the building and onto the grounds; the late afternoon sun was laying long golden shadows across the lawns. They walked together as far as the main house, then he paused, ready to turn down one of the other paths.

"I'll see you tomorrow then," he said lightly.

"OK. It was great meeting you—I enjoyed the practice."

He smiled at her tightly. "Same."

At that moment a boy came walking up the path. He was fairly tall and had dark, curly hair. Kirsten saw dimples form in his cheeks when he recognized Peter. His brown eyes sparkled as he stopped beside them.

"How're you doing, buddy?" the boy asked, grinning. "I was just on my way to meet some of the other guys from Trilling. We're getting together to play and fool around." He glanced at Kirsten, then to Peter. "You're not just getting through with rehearsal, are you? I heard Caldfrey call you up front. Problems?"

"No. He made some suggestions for our playing together. We were just practicing." Peter paused. "Terry, this is Kirsten Page. Kirsten, Terry McCormick, my roommate here and at Trilling, and a real good friend."

Kirsten smiled at Terry. "Nice to meet you."

Terry lifted his eyebrows. "Same here. I recognized you from introductions this morning. Glad to have you here for the summer. Too bad you got tied up with this deadhead, though." He winked at Kirsten to show he was teasing. "You don't know him at Trilling. Barely pays attention to anything but music and his stomach. I've never known him to leave our place except to walk a couple of blocks for pizza or a hamburger or to go to Lincoln Center or Carnegie Hall for a concert."

Kirsten threw Peter an alarmed glance, wondering if he was upset by his friend's words. Peter only shrugged and smiled. She liked his smile. "Bug off, Terry. I'm doing what I want, and I don't get on your case about all your late nights."

"True, you don't see me hanging around a practice room every free hour of the day. I get out and have a good time once in a while, but it's certainly not hurting my flute playing or the rest of my courses."

"You're going after something different than I am."

"Yeah, I'd rather work with a group than do the solo bit." Suddenly he laughed. "Will you listen to us? We're probably boring Kirsten to death."

Peter smiled, too. "We do this all the time," he explained. "Don't take it seriously."

"What are friends for, anyway?" Terry added. He glanced at his watch. "Well, got to go. Good to meet you, Kirsten. Be seeing more of you. Hey, Peter, you want to come with me?"

"Thanks, but I've got to go over some stuff."

"See what I mean?" Terry looked heavenward in mock exasperation. "All work and no play."

"Get out of here." Peter shoved Terry's shoulder good-naturedly. "See you back at the room."

"Bye, Kirsten." Terry gave her a wide smile, then swung off down the path, whistling to himself.

"He's a character," Peter said.

"He seemed nice."

"Yeah, well, he is."

There was a moment of awkward silence. Kirsten tried to think of something to say, anything that would draw out their conversation. His eyes briefly met hers, then he looked away. "Well, I've got to get going. See you tomorrow," he said quickly. With a wave of his hand, he turned and strode off.

Kirsten stood still for several moments watching him. She felt a strange excitement. She didn't know what to make of him or her reactions to him. He certainly was like no boy she'd ever met before. So quiet and self-contained that even his friend teased him about it. Yet there seemed to be something soft beneath that cool exterior, and he was as intensely involved in his music as she was.

She shook her head at these thoughts. She was really letting her imagination run wild. After all, she'd just met him. She barely knew him. *Ridiculous thoughts*, she scoffed.

At group rehearsal the next day Kirsten, standing beside the piano, found herself searching the crowd entering the hall, looking for Peter's blond head. She finally spotted him as he entered through a side door. She watched him walk to the stage and slide into his chair. As

Kirsten took her seat at the piano bench, she saw him glance over. He dropped his head quickly, but not before Kirsten saw what she thought was a warm smile on his lips.

Mr. Caldfrey, standing at the podium, tapped his baton a few times to get attention. Once they began playing, Kirsten was able to think of nothing but the music. But every time they took a break, her thoughts drifted back to Peter. She realized just how much she was looking forward to their rehearsal that evening. *What an idiot I am to get so carried away with this guy*, she thought to herself. *I've only just met him, and he probably has absolutely no interest in me. Why should he? He's so involved in his music, he probably has no time for girls.* Yet she couldn't stop hoping.

At the end of rehearsal Kirsten was surprised to see Mr. Caldfrey again motioning to her and Peter to join him at the podium.

"I must say," he said kindly, "that I'm impressed with the improvement you two have made already. Excellent. Of course, there's more work to be done."

"Yes, we realize that," Peter put in.

"Good, but what I had in mind when I called you over was to suggest another piece you might work on together. Our end-of-the-season performances are not at all set: we've left openings to be filled in with chamber groups and ensembles that have worked together over the summer. I was considering the two of you doing a duet. What do you think?"

Kirsten couldn't believe it. What an opportunity, both musical and—was a romance with Peter too much to hope for?

Kirsten was the first to speak. "That's quite a privilege. I'd be thrilled."

"And what about you, Peter?"

"Of course!"

"Wonderful." Mr. Caldfrey smiled. "I have some music here." He continued speaking as he leafed through the sheets in front of him. "You're both familiar with this piece, I believe. Why don't you start working on it, and I'll sit in with you later this week."

Kirsten scanned the score. She nodded to herself, then looked at the conductor. "Thank you very much. I'll start on it today."

"So will I," Peter said.

"Then I'll see you both tomorrow at rehearsal. Practice hard," he added sternly.

When he'd gone Peter spoke seriously, almost to himself. "He's giving us a real chance. We can't afford to blow it."

"I don't have any intention of blowing it." Kirsten's tone was more vehement than she'd intended, and Peter grinned at her determined expression.

"Don't worry. I'll be out there with you, too."

"I know. I didn't mean to sound so strong—it's just such a surprise."

"You can say that again. We have a lot of work to do." Suddenly Peter seemed a little self-conscious. "We can start going through it tonight."

"Good. I'll see if I can squeeze in some time later this afternoon to run through my part." Then, for no reason she could explain, she reached out and took his hand in a firm clasp. "Guess we're going to be partners for a while. Let's shake on it."

He was silent as her blue eyes met his. When she withdrew her hand and began to turn away, she barely heard his quiet, "I'm looking forward to working with you."

Chapter Five

Their practice session that evening went well. Much to Kirsten's delight, Peter loosened up a little. And in response to her coaxing questions, he told her more about himself.

"There are five kids in my family, and my parents are pretty strict—believe in all the old values. They love us, I know, but they see things only their way—especially my father, and he's not into music."

"Didn't they give you any encouragement? You're so talented, they must have realized."

"My mother does. When my father used to complain that I should be out doing something useful instead of playing my violin, my mother would run interference. I don't know what she'd say," he said, a grin starting to form, "but after she talked to him, he'd just mumble something and leave me alone. My brother and sisters thought I was weird, too, to sit in my room and practice rather than go down to the playground with them. Even now my father hasn't changed his mind. He thinks I'm crazy to try to make a living in music. He says I should put my mind to something realistic, a real trade."

"Does it bother you?"

"It used to. Sometimes it still hurts. The only one I could really talk to was the old man next door, Mr. Petrie. He could see my point of view. That's one of the reasons I was so glad to get to go to Trilling—and up here. I finally feel like I belong. Guess you never had that kind of problem."

"No," Kirsten said honestly. "My parents are behind me one hundred percent, but we aren't rich either, you know, and sometimes it's been hard on them to come up with the money for my lessons, but I help out baby-sitting when I can. But I do know about wanting to belong."

"I worked to pay for my lessons, too. At least at Trilling I'm on a full scholarship, I mean everything, so I can spend all my time on my music."

"Didn't you ever feel like you were missing

things—I mean putting all your energy into music and working?"

He seemed puzzled. "No. What was there to miss?"

"Going out with other kids—parties, football games, that kind of stuff."

"I wasn't very friendly with most of the kids in high school. We didn't have anything in common. Most of the time they thought I was strange."

She laughed. "I don't think you're strange—a little aloof and quiet—but OK." Kirsten's cheeks flushed. Maybe she was telling him too much. He did seem embarrassed. He hurriedly dropped his eyes and started rosining his bow as though he needed to have something to do with his hands. She hurried on to cover the awkward moment. "I don't have much in common with the kids at school, either. I found that out for sure at a dance we had just before I came up here. This one guy I was dancing with looked at me like I was from outer space when I told him I hadn't heard the new Journey album." She grinned, and Peter smiled back at her.

"Don't feel bad. Neither have I, though I'm sure Terry could tell you all about it."

"Yeah, he seems like the type of person who'd be up on everything that's the latest."

"You can say that again. At Trilling he's always off at some jazz or rock show. He meets tons of people, too, not like me."

"Everybody's different. There are talkers, and there are listeners."

"You trying to make me feel better because you said I was aloof?"

"Did it bother you?"

"I guess, but it is true. I suppose I've never really cared what other people thought. I had my music, and that was all that was important."

During the next three or four days, Kirsten and Peter's practice sessions would sometimes last late into the evenings. He got into the habit of coming to stand behind her as they worked, looking over her shoulder. It should have made her nervous, but it didn't. In fact, it was actually more comfortable for her than facing him. Several times during practice sessions, she had looked up from her music to find him staring at her, that serious look on his face.

With his standing directly behind her, however, he was right there to point out any slipups. He'd put his arm over her shoulder, his finger indicating the sheet of music.

"No, Kirsten, that passage should be lento."

"Well, you speeded it up the last time we went through it."

"I was experimenting."

"Oh? And it's all right for you to experiment, but not me?"

"That's not what I meant."

"What did you mean?"

"Never mind. Let's just do it lento. It sounds better that way."

"If you've ever listened to Mehta's New York Philharmonic recording of this, you'd know he picks up the tempo."

"I don't care what Zubin Mehta does."

Kirsten shook her head. Peter's confidence was absolutely amazing. It never would have occurred to her to question an acknowledged master.

"I'm sorry, Kirsten," he said, moving to sit beside her on the bench. "I didn't mean to sound so bossy. You were doing fine. It's just that I get these ideas, and I can't change them."

She smiled. "I'm beginning to understand your temperament—artistic all the way."

He looked directly at her. His smile was full of warmth, and for the first time he didn't turn away.

Chapter Six

Within the first few days at Greenacres, Kirsten, Rene, and Sharlie had gotten to know quite a few of their fellow students. Rene acted as a catalyst, bringing people together. That first Sunday after they arrived, she organized a group to go into the nearby town of Stoneham to explore for the morning. They all wanted to attend that afternoon's concert so the expedition had to be a quick one.

It was a mixed and lively crowd that set out from Greenacres's grounds on foot. Terry McCormick was one of the boys, and he came up to Kirsten as she was walking beside Sharlie.

"Hi, there, Kirsten," he said, grinning.

"Well, hello. How are you?"

"Fine. Haven't talked to you in a few days. How's it going? Still like Greenacres?"

"It's fun—work, too, of course—but I'm really glad I came." Kirsten motioned to Sharlie. "Terry, I'd like you to meet my roommate. This is Sharlie Watson. Sharlie, Terry McCormick."

Terry's grin deepened, showing his dimples. "Hi, Sharlie." He glanced down at her with definite interest.

Sharlie, shy as ever, managed a tiny but charming smile. "Hello, Terry."

"You play the cello, don't you?" he asked.

Sharlie nodded self-consciously, and Terry, sensing her shyness, turned to Kirsten. "Guess you're wondering where Peter is."

"I bet I can guess—working."

"You got it. That guy never gives himself a break. I thought this summer might change things but. . . ." He threw up his hands.

"The summer's not over yet."

"No, that's true. You got something in mind? I know Peter thinks a lot of you."

"Does he?" Kirsten couldn't stop the blush from rising to her cheeks.

"Well, you know, he never says too much about what he's thinking, but I get these signals."

"I'm sure it's just because we're working together on a couple of pieces. It's going well."

"So he says—high praise from the master, by the way."

"I'll have to thank him."

"No! Don't do that!" Terry cried. "He'd have a fit if he knew I was talking to you about him."

"In that case I won't say a word."

"Thanks."

Kirsten noticed Terry was again looking at Sharlie. She decided it wouldn't hurt to leave them alone to get better acquainted.

As nonchalantly as possible, she said, "I have to talk to Rene about something. She's at the front of the group. Can you keep Sharlie company for a while, Terry?"

"I sure can."

Kirsten hoped Sharlie didn't notice Terry's sly wink.

As Kirsten stepped away, he immediately moved to Sharlie's side. "So," Kirsten heard him say, "tell me more about yourself. Where're you from? How're your mom and dad? Any sisters or brothers? Who do you think will win the pennant? Do you have a date for the concert this afternoon?"

Kirsten laughed in spite of herself; she could see that Terry would be good for Sharlie. She was disappointed and a little sad that Peter wasn't a part of the group. She hadn't said anything to him about the expedition, since it had been a last-minute arrangement, but Terry must have mentioned it that morning. If Peter was at all interested in her, wouldn't he have come along just to see if she was there? Well, he *was* different, Kirsten tried to console herself, and his dedication to music did take precedence over everything else. He probably didn't know how to have fun. During their rehearsals together, she'd allowed herself to think that he liked her, that he saw her as a girl and not just as the pianist he happened to be working with. It would be awful if she'd been wrong about that—especially since it was the first time she'd had a relationship with a boy that she wanted to build into something more serious.

Perhaps she'd see him at the concert that afternoon, she thought, although it would be unlikely because so many people attended the concerts, and judging by the number of people in town already, it would be a big crowd. She sighed and forced her thoughts to the back of her mind.

She looked around the picturesque little streets of Stoneham. It was a cute town, mainly a tourist stop with small individualized shops and genuine New England colonials lining the roads. She and Rene paired off. Kirsten had to smile a few minutes later as Rene poked her in the ribs and glanced back at Terry and Sharlie walking together.

"What's going on back there? I never thought she'd get up the courage to talk to a guy."

"They're hitting it off pretty well, aren't they?" Kirsten agreed. "Terry's Peter's roommate. He seemed kind of interested in Sharlie, so I left them alone."

"Couldn't have done better myself. Good for Sharlie. She needs someone to help her open up. Hope he's not just playing around."

Frowning, Kirsten shook her head. "No, I don't think so. And if he were playing around, I don't think he'd pick out someone as introverted as Sharlie. He doesn't seem the type, and Peter thinks the world of him."

"Oh, yeah? By the way, where's Peter? I was hoping the two of you might get something going."

"Terry tells me he's working this morning."

"That guy doesn't know when to quit, does he? He's got the orchestra scores down perfectly, he plays beautifully—he's absolutely killing the rest of us." Rene stopped in front of a shop window. "Oh! Will you look at this super store. Let's go in. I've got a few bucks, and I want to get some souvenirs for my family."

As they stepped into the crowded store, Rene picked up her conversation where she'd left off.

"Not that I don't admire Peter. It gives me goose bumps to listen to him—and, of course, looking at him's even better! Do you know how lucky you are to get to play with him?"

"I thank my fairy godmother every night," Kirsten said and giggled. "Not that it's going to get me anywhere."

"Don't be too sure about that. He's always looking at you during rehearsals."

Kirsten flushed. "You must be imagining things."

"I almost wish I were. I'm jealous as anything! Just wait and see," she said as she picked up a painted plate showing a scene of Stoneham. "This would be perfect for my mother, and I can even afford it."

Although Kirsten looked for Peter at the concert Sunday afternoon, she didn't see him; there were just too many people. She shared a blanket with Rene and two college girls who were in a room two doors down from them. Sharlie had gone to the concert with Terry, and Kirsten felt a pang of envy; she wished that she could have been with Peter.

There was an orchestra rehearsal Monday morning, and although Peter smiled at her when she came in, he made no move to talk to her.

That evening Peter was already in the rehearsal

room when Kirsten arrived. He was standing near the window, looking out. He turned as soon as he heard the door open and smiled.

Kirsten returned his smile happily, her stomach doing a flip-flop. "You're early."

"I got bored sitting around the room. Terry's out jamming with some of the guys. He asked me to sit in, but I told him I was meeting you."

"Would you rather have gone with them? We can always make up the practice another night."

"No." It was all he said, but the way he looked at her made Kirsten's heart start to pound. She walked quickly to the piano.

"Terry tells me that he saw you yesterday when you went into town and then to the concert."

"We had a good time. Did you get to the concert?"

"I got there late. I didn't know you were going into town. You didn't say anything Friday."

"It was kind of a last-minute thing."

"Oh. How'd you like Stoneham?"

"Pretty town. But how did you like the Mozart? Wasn't it the best?"

Peter smiled faintly.

She didn't know if he hadn't liked the music or if he was distracted.

He took his bow from the case. "Well, maybe next time you all get together, I'll come along. I—I'd like to see some of the area."

So, he had really wanted to go with them. "Sure. That woud be great! I guess you never got to travel much," she added as an afterthought.

"Unless you call a trip to New York City to see Trilling traveling. To my folks the world begins and ends in New Jersey. Their adventures are limited to the TV set. Oh, when I was little, we went to a couple of amusement parks, but my mom and dad were always too broke or too tired to do much else. They both worked. We all worked when we were old enough. I got a job in a music store, and they weren't too happy about that, at least my father wasn't. I could have made more money at the plant where he worked, assembling computer circuits, but I would have gone crazy."

How different Peter's life had been from hers, Kirsten thought. Although her family wasn't rich, by any stretch of the imagination, once a year they went off on a vacation—camping in the mountains or swimming at the beach. One year they took a trip to Washington, D.C. and Williamsburg. She always looked forward to their summer vacations.

"Since I started at Trilling," Peter continued, "Terry's got me traveling a lot more. He can't stand to see me sitting around studying and practicing all the time. Thinks I'm going to turn into a block of wood or something." He laughed. "I guess you noticed."

Kirsten smiled.

"I'm not entirely a lost cause," Peter said more seriously. "Some of what he says sinks in. I know my attitude's too heavy. But I've always had to work so hard to get where I am, I'm afraid to slack off and maybe lose everything." He studied his hands. "I couldn't face going back home a failure—listening to all the I-told-you-so's."

Before she could stop herself, Kirsten reached out and placed her hand over his. She meant it only as a gesture of understanding, but Peter reacted as though she'd touched him with a hot coal. Yet just as she was about to withdraw her hand, he suddenly smiled and squeezed her fingers.

"You must think I'm a real complainer. I'm certainly not the only one to have it rough."

"Sometimes it's good to talk about it. And you've been up against more than I have, that's for sure. At least my parents have always been behind me."

She let her hand slip from his, but not before she saw his soft, encouraging smile. Their friendship had just progressed to a new level.

Kirsten found herself thinking more and more about Peter. She'd catch herself in the middle of orchestra rehearsal daydreaming, barely bringing her mind back to attention for a new direction. Was it only her imagination, or did she catch Peter looking at her a lot? Was he softer when he spoke to her? Was he more open when they were alone together? Was she falling in love? Is that what the crazy, excited feeling inside her was?

It was a particularly hot afternoon, and Kirsten, Rene, and Sharlie decided to put on their swimsuits after classes and go down to the lake.

"Wow," Rene called as they emerged from the woods to cross the grassy area to the lake. "Some crowd here today. Look, there are Terry and Peter. Do you know the other two guys they're with?"

Sharlie had brightened immediately when Rene mentioned Terry's name, and Kirsten felt her heart jump as she glanced in the direction of Rene's pointing arm.

"I've seen them," Kirsten mused, "but don't know their names."

In the meantime Terry had spotted the girls and was waving vigorously for them to come over.

"Shall we?" Rene asked, teasing the other two.

"You bet." Sharlie giggled. "Do you even have to ask?"

Peter, whose back had been toward the girls, turned now and watched their approach. It was obvious that his eyes were for Kirsten alone.

"Hi, girls," Terry called. His greeting was for them all, but he was gravitating toward Sharlie. "Decided to beat the heat like the rest of us? This is Steve Warner and Mike Bell." He indicated the two boys the girls hadn't recognized. "Steve and Mike, Rene Schulman, Sharlie Watson, and Kirsten Page."

They all exchanged hellos.

"Well," said Terry cheerfully, "you ready for a swim?"

It seemed only natural as they all moved in the direction of the water that Peter should end up at Kirsten's side. "Hi." He spoke quietly, but it was obvious he was glad to see her.

"Hi." Kirsten's voice was quiet, too. She'd never seen Peter in a swimsuit before. The sight of his tall, well-proportioned body made her feel shy.

"You like to swim?" he asked.

"Yes, but I'm not great at it." She nodded her head toward two guys doing graceful crawls and cutting through the water like knives. "I never could manage that—always seem to be opening my mouth for a breath at the wrong time and getting a mouthful of water instead."

He laughed.

"But I can get by. What about you?"

"I'm a pretty good swimmer, I guess. It was one of those things I could do without having to join a team, and there was a Y in town right down the street from our building."

They'd slowly waded in until they were waist deep. Most of the others, however, had wasted no time getting in and were already in the middle of a water fight.

"Doesn't look like I'm going to be able to get wet a little at a time," Kirsten said, laughing as she got splashed.

"Sure doesn't," Peter agreed. "Come on." He took her hand. "We might as well join them."

Kirsten had no time to protest as he pulled her forward, diving into the water himself and leaving her to follow a second later. He emerged through the surface several yards ahead of her, paused for a moment until he spotted her, then swam with strong, sure strokes back to her.

There's no question that he's a great swimmer, Kirsten thought, feeling self-conscious about her own inability.

As he stopped to tread water beside her, Terry called over to them. "We're going to have a game of water tag. Come on over and join us."

Kirsten saw Peter hesitate. She knew from his expression that he would enjoy the game, but in a second he shook his head.

"Thanks, Terry, but we're playing lazy today."

"That's not allowed! You'll miss all the fun."

"Kirsten and I are having our own fun."

"Oh, yeah?" Kirsten could see the teasing twinkle in Terry's eyes.

"Can it, Terry," Peter said, laughing. "Get on with your game. Maybe we'll join you later."

When Terry's attention was directed back to his fellow players, Kirsten spoke to Peter. "I hope you didn't say you wouldn't play on my account."

"No." His smile was sincere. "I really do feel lazy. Besides I'd rather be with you."

The words took Kirsten totally by surprise. "You—you would?"

"Sure. I thought you understood—" Peter suddenly realized what he was saying and blushed. Quickly he said, "Let's swim for a while. I'll take it slow."

"OK—fine—but I'm not that bad, you know."

"I didn't say you were."

He set off doing a sidestroke, and Kirsten swam along beside him. He seemed tongue-tied now, so Kirsten broke the silence.

"Do you come down here to swim often?"

"Nearly every day."

"Funny I've never seen you."

"Well, I usually come when no one else is around, swim a bit, and go back to my room."

"And I thought all you did was practice," she teased.

He grinned. "See, I keep a few secrets from the rest of you. Actually I have to get away from the music once in a while, and coming down here for a swim helps to get rid of the tension."

"You're really a good swimmer."

"Do you think so?"

"Yes, your style's great."

Again he was self-conscious. "I never thought much about my style—only enjoyed swimming."

They swam in comfortable silence. After a while Kirsten was winded. To give herself time to catch her breath, she rolled over on her back to float, kicking her legs occasionally to keep herself moving very slightly through the water. Although her eyes were staring up at the sky, she could sense Peter's nearness, feel the ripples caused by his movements. It was good to know he was lazily floating beside her and even better to remember his earlier words: he'd said he wanted to be with her.

She was interrupted from her daydream by the pressure of his fingers on her arm. With her ears below water, she hadn't heard him speaking to her.

Quickly she righted herself to tread water—so quickly, in fact, that she found her shoulder brushing up against his chest, her face only a few inches from his. They stared at each other, both startled by the unexpected closeness of their bodies. She saw his lips move just the tiniest bit, parting slightly. She didn't breathe, only watched his mouth, her heart beating rapidly. He was going to kiss her, she was sure of it. And, oh, how she wanted him to! Her own lips trembled in anticipation.

Then suddenly the magic of the moment was shattered as they both became aware of their surroundings.

"I—I—" He cleared his throat. "I just wanted to tell you that we've gone pretty far. We should turn back."

"Um—OK, you're right."

"Are you tired?"

"No."

"You might be by the time we get back. We'll go slowly."

"All right." Her voice was hushed. She couldn't get the image of Peter almost kissing her out of her mind.

They said nothing to each other until they were near the shore. The other kids had left the water and were now involved in a loud game of volleyball in the nearby clearing.

"Want to sit in the sun for a while?" Peter asked as they walked out of the water. "You look cold."

Kirsten glanced down at the goose bumps on her arms and knew they weren't from feeling cold. But she wasn't ready to join the other kids either.

"That sounds good."

They spread their towels and plopped down on their stomachs. Again they were silent. Peter reached over and broke off a few blades of grass, toying with them in his long, well-shaped fingers, his attention concentrated on his hands. His eyes remained downcast as he spoke.

"When Terry asked me to come, I was hoping you'd be here."

"I was glad to see you, too."

"I've never paid much attention to girls. I mean, I notice a pretty face as fast as the next guy, but girls didn't have any part in my plans. Dating would have gotten in the way of my goals." He paused.

Kirsten said nothing—she didn't know what to say.

"But you're different. I noticed it right from the start. It's not just the music. You understand me. You—"

Whatever else he was going to say was cut off

as the volleyball came bouncing madly out of the clearing, headed directly toward them.

Peter jumped up and caught the ball as Rene came running in pursuit.

"Hey, thanks, Peter. I was sure I'd have to go swimming to get it back. And what are you two doing lying around over here? You got away with that once today, but not again. Come on over and join the game. We need more players."

Kirsten desperately wanted to hear the rest of what Peter had intended to say, but she knew that after the interruption they'd never be able to pick up the conversation where they'd left off. She glanced at Peter.

He shrugged. "Do you feel like playing, Kirsten? I'm willing."

"So am I."

"OK, let's go." He looked at Rene. "By the way, who hit that last ball? Just a little off target."

She grinned sheepishly. "I did, who do you think? Why else would I be chasing it?" And as Peter raised his brows she added, "So, I'm a violinist, not a volleyball player."

That night Kirsten couldn't sleep. She lay in bed thinking over and over about the events of the afternoon. What did it all mean?

"Rene," she whispered. "You still awake?"

"Yeah."

"Sharlie asleep?"

"Sure sounds like it."

"Have you ever been kissed, Rene?"

"Once, though it wasn't very good. My date for the junior prom sort of took my shoulders and plopped one on my lips. Can't say it left me in ecstasy like you see in those old movies."

"I was wondering because I think Peter almost kissed me today."

"Really? You only *think* he tried to kiss you? Couldn't you tell?"

"Well, we were out in the water, and we sort of bumped into each other, and he had this look on his face. I was so sure. Then all of a sudden he seemed to change his mind—said we ought to head in."

"Hmmm, sounds promising."

"Do you think? And later when we were sitting on the grass, he said some pretty nice things. If you hadn't come over chasing the ball—"

"Sorry about that. My timing was really rotten."

"You didn't know. It's just that I have so little experience with boys—none in fact—that I don't know whether I'm crazy and just imagining things."

"You definitely aren't imagining things. The way he hung around you all day today—just have a little patience."

"I will. Thanks, Rene. Good night."

But Kirsten still couldn't sleep. She stared up at the ceiling, wondering, wishing. *I hope Rene's right*, she thought. *Maybe if I wait just a little longer. . . .*

Chapter Seven

It was really hard to do at times, but Kirsten tried to be patient for the next few days, hoping for another intimate moment between herself and Peter. Peter was warm and friendly and obviously glad to see her when they met, but he didn't talk about his feelings, and he didn't try to kiss her again.

Their work together was going so smoothly that they didn't need to rehearse every day anymore; yet, neither brought up the subject. Kirsten kept thinking Peter might be ready to suggest an end to their everyday rehearsals; he certainly wasn't the kind to waste time. It was getting hard to think of excuses to continue going through pieces that were already perfect.

One evening after they'd run through everything flawlessly in less than an hour, Kirsten tried desperately to prolong their session.

"You've never told me much about the chamber group you're in, Peter. You'll be performing with them at the end-of-the-season concerts as well as doing our duet?"

"Yes, though I think I'm getting more out of what you and I are doing together." His eyes met hers quickly, then moved away.

"That's nice of you to say."

"I mean it."

Both were silent, awkward, searching for words.

"Mr. Caldfrey seemed happy when he listened to us yesterday," Kirsten said finally.

Peter nodded. "He told me he didn't think we needed to work on our pieces any more, just keep them polished."

Kirsten sighed. The words she'd been dreading couldn't be avoided forever. "I guess, then, we don't need to meet every night." Her voice quivered, although she tried to keep it firm.

The expression on Peter's face wasn't readable. "Are you glad?"

"No—"

"Kirsten—" But then he changed his mind, and instead of speaking, he brought his violin up to his chin, turned his back on her, and began to play.

It was a song Kirsten had never heard before. A beautiful melody filled the room, crying out with an intensity that left Kirsten stunned.

As the song reached its climax, he swung around to face her, his bow sweeping across the strings, coaxing music from his instrument as though it were a living thing. While the last notes still reverberated in the air, Peter moved quickly to her side, staring down into her eyes.

"That was beautiful," she whispered. "I—I've never heard it before."

"I wrote it." He spoke so quietly that if the room hadn't been absolutely silent, she wouldn't have heard him.

"I didn't know you composed."

"Yes—for some time."

"I see." Kirsten didn't know what else to say.

"Kirsten." He set his violin down beside the piano. "I wrote it for you."

"For me?"

"Yes." Quickly, as though he were acting on an impulse he was afraid would desert him, he reached down and drew her up from the piano bench. They stood facing each other. "I don't know how to put things into words very well. I've never felt this way about a girl before. I knew these practice meetings would be ending soon. I didn't know if I would get to see you alone again, and I wanted you to know how I felt—so I wrote this song."

She was so thrilled, so surprised, her knees suddenly felt unable to support her.

"Is it OK?" His tone was pleading, uncertain.

"OK? It's wonderful. It's what I've been wishing for."

Peter's face lit up. He drew her into his arms. Then he was kissing her—not an experienced kiss, but a warm and tender one. She felt herself trembling with excitement. She'd never imagined her first kiss would be so wonderful!

He spoke softly into her ear. "This has never happened to me. I feel like I'm dreaming."

"So do I," she said breathlessly. "But I'm happy."

"I was afraid you didn't feel the same way I did."

"I was afraid, too. I've never really dated. All my time's gone into the piano and schoolwork. I didn't know how to act—"

He smiled to himself. "And here I thought you had a string of boyfriends at home."

"And I thought you were so involved with your music, you didn't want anything to do with girls. I thought I was crazy to like you so much."

"Oh, Kirsten, I'm so glad I met you. Will you

meet me tomorrow night? We can go to the concert together. It's all Beethoven."

"I'd love that."

There's so much more I want to know about you."

"You're so quiet. You never let anyone see beneath your surface."

"Maybe you can start changing that. Show me what I've been missing."

"I'll try." She looked up at him, and again he pressed his lips to hers, shyly, tenderly.

Chapter Eight

Kirsten found it impossible to sleep that night. She was so filled with happiness, she replayed every moment of the evening over and over again. She stared out the window at the star-spattered sky, her mind whirling, a soft smile on her lips. She was afraid to believe it had happened. Peter cared for her! He'd kissed her! *This is how Cinderella must have felt when the prince danced with her,* she thought, remembering the feel of his lips. Her first kiss, and it was everything she had hoped it would be. Just the thought of it brought a warm tingle—and in a few hours she would see him again. It would be at orchestra rehearsal, and they wouldn't be able to say more than hi, but there was their date after dinner to look forward to. There was so much she wanted to talk to him about.

She finally dozed off in the early morning, yet despite her lack of sleep, she woke up full of energy and anticipation for the day ahead.

She hummed to herself as she dressed. Rene, as usual grouchy in the morning, shot a look at Sharlie.

"Will you get a load of her—Miss Cheerful! And it's not even eight-thirty."

Kirsten laughed. "Just because you're a crab in the morning doesn't mean the rest of us are."

"You're going at it with a little too much energy, don't you think?" Rene continued to grumble as she pulled a T-shirt over her head.

"Go splash some water on your face," Kirsten said, teasing, "so you can bounce back to your usual bright and happy self."

"Humph." Rene snorted as she left for the bathroom.

"What I want to know," she asked when she'd returned, "is what's so great about this morning? We don't usually hear you singing away."

"Oh, nothing," Kirsten answered innocently. "I'm just in a good mood today."

Rene's eyes narrowed speculatively. "Something happen last night we should know about?

Now that I think of it, you had a smug little grin on your face when you came in."

"No—" But Kirsten's twinkling eyes gave her away.

"Come on—out with it! It's got something to do with Peter, right? What happened?"

"He just asked me to go to the concert tonight."

"*Just!* Do you believe this roommate of ours, Sharlie? She pulls off the impossible and acts like it's no big deal!"

"I didn't say it was no big deal. As a matter of fact, I'm thrilled."

"I would be, too! So what else happened? What did he say?"

"We talked for a while. He—he kissed me."

"Oo-ee!" Rene shrieked.

"Now wait," Kirsten laughingly protested, but Rene was off on a tangent and couldn't be stopped.

"Mr. Aloof himself!"

"It's true, Kirsten," Sharlie added. "Terry told me how Peter barely even looks at girls. His music's everything."

"What did I tell you," Rene said, wagging her finger.

"I know, but you guys are jumping to conclusions. He asked me to see him tonight—that's all. It may not mean anything."

"Yeah, you're right," Rene conceded, at the

same time giving Sharlie a conspiratorial wink. "Probably doesn't mean a thing. Hey, it's getting late. Let's go get some breakfast before they clear the tables."

As the girls entered the rehearsal hall forty-five minutes later, Kirsten unconsciously looked toward Peter's chair. It was empty, and he was always on time, usually early. It wasn't until Mr. Caldfrey was walking toward his podium that Peter came hurrying in. He didn't look toward Kirsten as he went to his seat. She couldn't help but feel a moment's anxiety. Was last night all a mistake? she wondered. Maybe he hadn't meant it after all.

Mr. Caldfrey called the orchestra to attention, and Kirsten didn't realize Peter was watching her. Finally he caught her eye and smiled. A current of excitement passed silently between them.

Kirsten waited impatiently for lunch break, hoping she'd have a chance to talk to Peter, but when Mr. Caldfrey announced recess, a couple of the other kids called Peter over. He glanced quickly in her direction and shrugged before turning his attention to Jim Dawson, one of the high-school seniors, who played the violin. He obviously had questions about the score.

She had no choice but to leave with the rest of the crowd. She met Rene outside on the lawn. Kirsten watched the exit doors carefully, only listening with half an ear to Rene's conversation, but Peter didn't appear. Too soon it was time to go back in. He wasn't in his chair, either, but as Kirsten sat down at the piano, she noticed a folded sheet of music on top of her other arrangements. Curious, she picked it up and unfolded it. It was a brief handwritten score. At the bottom left-hand corner of the sheet was scrawled "Peter."

Before the others settled into their seats, she quietly picked out the melody. It was light and cheerful, like a sparkling spring morning. Her heart beating rapidly, she stashed the music in her bag and looked over to the violin section. He was there, watching her, obviously awaiting her reaction.

She winked at him, He grinned back, then shyly looked away. Kirsten knew what she was going to do.

That afternoon before her private class, she went to one of the empty rehearsal sheds. She didn't have Peter's gift for composing music, but she would try her best. It was the thought that counted. The results weren't as spectacular as she would have liked, but by the end of an hour, she'd created a little song that described at least some of her feelings. *I'll give it to him this evening,* she thought excitedly.

*   *   *

Peter was waiting as she stepped out the front door of her dorm at exactly seven-thirty. He was leaning against a maple tree beside the walk, holding a blanket. When he saw her, he stepped forward a little awkwardly.

Trying to put him at ease, Kirsten gave him a happy wave and hurried down the steps. "Hi, Peter. Have you been waiting long? I'm probably late."

"No, I just got here. You look nice."

"Thank you." She'd changed her clothes three times before she left, finally settling on a blue and green print skirt, a light blue camisole top, and a white lace shawl. Her dark hair shone, curling softly to her shoulders.

She started down the path, and he fell into step beside her. "It's such a nice night. Do you want to go into town after the concert? I've never been there."

"I don't think there'll be time."

As they moved away from the buildings, following a path under the trees, Kirsten spoke quietly. "Thank you for the music, Peter. I really liked it."

Self-consciously he reached for her hand and squeezed it gently, then continued to hold it. "I wrote it last night when I got home."

"I've got something for you, too, but I'm not going to give it to you until later."

"Going to keep me wondering?"

"Only for a while."

"I guess I can wait. How did your class go after rehearsal?"

"Couldn't have been better. But the best part of the day was what was waiting for me before that after lunch." Kirsten noticed Peter blush. "How was your class?"

"Hard, but I like the work. Ms. Mansard pushes me beyond what I think I can do." He paused. "I've been thinking, Kirsten. Does it bother you that I've always been so much of a loner? Until last night I never realized how out of it I've been."

"It doesn't bother me, and I don't think you're out of it. You've just been wrapped up in music."

"Yeah."

"I understand. My music has been everything to me, too," she said quietly.

"But that's different," he said curtly.

"Different how?" Kirsten was puzzled. He hadn't missed out on any more than she had, and her devotion to her music wasn't any less than his.

He shrugged. "Just different."

He didn't seem to want to talk, and Kirsten didn't want to push. They had reached the lawn in front of the stage and began looking for a place. "Another full house," Kirsten said, looking around at the crowd. "Or should I say 'another full lawn'?"

Peter laughed. "Somehow, that just doesn't sound right."

Directly in front of them sat a couple with two children. The boy knocked over the girl's glass of lemonade, and she began to scream.

"Let's find a place away from kids," Peter said. "I've had enough of that kind of stuff at home."

"Me, too!" Kirsten emphatically agreed. "We can sit off to the side. We'll be able to hear from anywhere."

They found a place, and as they spread the blanket, the sounds of the orchestra warming up spilled out across the lawn.

As they sat down, Kirsten said, "I'm really excited about the Beethoven piano concerto. I've never had the nerve to try it. Mr. Jennings, my piano teacher, says I'm ready, but I'm a coward."

"I'm sure you could do it," Peter said.

They lay down on their backs, looking up at the sky and waiting for the concert to begin. "I want to see what you've got for me," Peter said abruptly.

"You may be disappointed."

He looked over at her. "I don't think I will be."

With her eyes still on the sky, Kirsten responded a little breathlessly. "I hope not."

She sat up, took the folded music from her purse, and hesitantly handed it across to him. "You wouldn't be able to see it later, anyway," she said, after lying down again.

He didn't say anything, only sat up, unfolded the paper, and let his eyes scan the handwritten notes. Kirsten looked up at his profile, afraid he'd think her little song was silly. A tiny frown formed on his brow, then disappeared. He lay back down and reached for her hand.

"Thank you. It's beautiful."

"You really think so?" she asked, looking sideways at him. "I never tried to write anything before."

"That makes it even better—that you wrote your first piece of music for me." His voice was soft and sincere. He didn't let go of her hand as the musicians took their places on the stage.

The concert consisted of only two piece. Both were Beethoven's: the Concerto no. 3 for Piano and Orchestra and Symphony no. 2 in D major. Kirsten was moved to tears during the concerto, and both she and Peter shouted for more at the end of the symphony. Neither could speak during the walk back to Kirsten's dorm—the music and the star-filled sky had filled both of them with the magic and mystery of nature and the best of man.

In the shadow of one of the trees outside her dorm, Peter stopped and placed his hands gently on Kirsten's shoulders.

"It's been one of my very best nights ever, Kirsten. Thank you."

"Thank you."

"I'll see you tomorrow?"

"Yes."

"Tomorrow night, I mean."

"That's even better."

He pulled her close, his cheek resting against her hair as he whispered, "Oh, Kirsten." He found her lips for one long, soft kiss.

Chapter Nine

Kirsten walked around in a daze the next couple of weeks. Every evening she and Peter met, sometimes for a walk, sometimes just to sit and talk alone, and sometimes to attend one of the many musical events on the grounds.

Peter was less intense; he even teased and joked with the other kids. A very different side of his personality was emerging, a side no one had imagined existed.

Kirsten didn't realize how wonderful the change in him was until a group of them were walking into town early one evening for pizza. Peter and Kirsten were walking hand in hand, listening to the easy banter of the others and laughing.

"I really shouldn't be taking off to go into town like this," Terry remarked cheerfully. "Caldfrey really got on my case this afternoon— told me I had one day to get my flute solo right, or he'd personally chain me in a practice room and stand guard over me."

Peter laughed. "Yeah, I heard him. Might not be a bad idea."

"What do you mean?"

"Chain you up and have someone else do the fingering on your flute—probably sound a lot better."

"Hey, wait a minute—"

Sharlie grinned, jabbing him in the ribs. "I think he's teasing you, Terry."

Terry swung around to look at his friend's face.

Peter lifted his brows innocently.

Terry shook his head but was smiling now, too. "OK, guess I set that one up for you."

Whenever Kirsten and Peter were alone, he talked to her about his dreams.

"In three, maybe four, years I expect my life will be a lot different. By then I'll be finished with my training, except for regular lessons, of course. I hope I'll have made a name for myself through the student concerts, and I'll know better where I'm headed professionally. I just hope when I get there I'll be able to continue concentrating on the other parts of my life, too."

"What other parts?"

"Friendships, fun. Someday, when the worst of the struggle is over, there'll be time for other things. I *want* other things. It's because of you, Kirsten. You've helped me see that it's safe to open up to other people. Terry's helped, too, but meeting you has been really special." A shy flush rose on his cheeks. "You're just—I don't know how to say it—just the best."

That they never discussed her ambitions didn't bother Kirsten at that point. She realized that Peter had never had anyone his own age he could really talk to, and now he was letting everything out in a flood. She was happy that he cared enough for her to be able to confide in her.

They continued to exchange their musical letters: every few days Kirsten would find a folded sheet of music on her piano and slip her musical answer onto Peter's music stand. His little melodies were like love letters to her, and she read them again and again, carefully storing them away in her dresser drawer.

All their friends watched their romance with great interest. And even though Peter was still self-conscious, neither he nor Kirsten attempted to hide how they felt about each other.

Rene, of course, teased Kirsten good-naturedly. "I knew something was going to happen. Between you and Peter, and Sharlie and Terry—I'm beginning to feel really left out."

"Don't be silly. And I've seen you talking to that guy who plays bass."

"Oh, Steve? That's only because we're in the chamber group together."

"Sure about that?"

"Well—" Rene grinned. "Too bad all of this is only for the summer."

Kirsten felt the same way. She was afraid to look too far ahead, knowing that in about a month Peter would be back at Trilling and she'd be in Fairly. She was dreading the school year ahead—her senior year, supposedly the best. She forced it to the back of her mind and tried to think of one day at a time.

Although Peter was attentive and thoughtful, it was still difficult for him to express his feelings. Kirsten's pride told her that she should wait for him to bring up the subject of continuing their relationship. She knew that the feeling between them was deepening, and she knew that for the first time in her life she was in love.

Although there was no longer any need for them to meet for practice sessions, they did often go to a rehearsal shed to play together just for fun. As she listened to Peter playing her latest musical letter one night, she thought how much better it sounded when he brought it to life on his strings and how accurately he'd caught the emotion she'd intended.

He came to sit beside her on the piano bench. "Let's try it again. I like this the best of anything you've done. It has real possibilities."

Kirsten smiled. "You're sure you're not just trying to make me feel good?"

"You should know I don't hand out praise that easily," he said, laughing. "At least that's the reputation I hear I've gotten."

He really has come out of his shell if he can laugh at that, Kirsten thought.

Together they played Kirsten's melody through, and Kirsten had to admit that she was moved.

"Good." Peter nodded. "Excellent. We're a good team."

"I've known that for a while."

He reached over and took her hand. "So have I. Kirsten, I've been thinking about us—that the summer won't last forever. I don't want to say goodbye to you in September."

"I feel the same way, Peter. I'll miss you, but maybe we can work something out."

"You mean see each other."

"It's not that far from Fairly to New York. You could come up for weekends and meet my family and Mr. Jennings, my piano teacher."

Peter's grip on her fingers tightened. "Sounds good to me. And maybe you could come to New York. I could take you through Trilling. You'll want to see it anyway since that's where you want to study."

"Getting to see you," Kirsten said with a smile, "is enough of an incentive to come down."

Peter's arm slipped around Kirsten's waist. She dropped her head on his shoulder, and Peter brushed his lips against her forehead. "Kirsten, you know I'm not very good at putting things into words. I just know that it's so good to be with you. I think about you all the time, look forward to seeing you, and when we're together everything seems so right—not just the music, but everything. I've never been sure what love was, but I think I know now. I love you, Kirsten."

"I love you, too."

"Do you mean it?"

"Yes, I mean it. I've been feeling all the things you have."

"But you're so pretty and friendly. You could have so many other guys. Are you really sure you care for me?"

"I never knew Peter Restrochek could lack confidence," she teased.

"Not in most things—this is different." His expression was so serious, so anxious.

"I don't want anyone else, Peter. You're the only guy I've known who likes me for who I am. I can't sit down and make music with other guys. I can't talk to them because we have nothing in common. You and I do."

He smiled then, very shyly, as he pulled her close. His mouth brushed hers in a gentle caress, then pressed more firmly, his lips moving warmly against hers. They were both breathless when he lifted his head and touched his lips to the tip of her nose. He gave a lopsided grin. "I'm almost afraid to believe this is happening. I'm so happy!"

"So am I," she whispered. "I never knew love could be so fantastic!"

"We'll make it even better!"

Chapter Ten

The world couldn't have been much brighter for Kirsten. Everything she'd been dreaming of had come true at Greenacres. She'd made good friends who shared her love for music and met a wonderful boy—and he loved her! Rene teased her about walking around ten feet off the ground.

As for Peter, everyone noticed the change in him. His new self was in complete contrast to the aloof, introverted one who'd arrived at Greenacres.

One Sunday after a piano recital, Rene arranged for a picnic. About twenty kids were to meet at the lake at four-thirty for swimming and games. The day was beautiful, warm, clear, with a slight breeze. Walking from the concert to the lake, Peter held Kirsten's hand and carried a bag filled with food in his other. Sharlie and Terry strolled along a few yards ahead of them, followed by Rene and Steve, who were deep in conversation. Every few minutes Peter and Kirsten would hear a burst of laughter.

"They're having a good time," Peter commented.

"Sounds like it. I'm having a good time, too."

"Mmmm." Peter squeezed her hand. "They're going to be calling us a couple of lovebirds pretty soon."

"They already are."

"No," Peter said with alarm. "I don't mean that I mind people thinking we're in love, it's just that I don't like them talking about us at all."

"I don't know why it should bother you," Kirsten replied, smiling. "You've been a topic of conversation around here since the day you arrived."

"*Me?*"

"It was that air of mystery about you."

"Oh, come on, Kirsten. You're putting me on."

"I'm telling you the absolute truth—but I'll also tell you that people like you better the way you are now."

Peter laughed. "Well, I'm glad to hear that. I like myself better, too."

They spread blankets in the grass near the lake's edge under a broad-limbed tree. Already some of the other kids were eating, swimming, or playing Frisbee.

"How about some disc before we eat?" shouted Terry. In a minute they were all out on the grassy field, the Frisbee whizzing between them.

"Terry," Sharlie called, "you know I couldn't reach that!"

"Run for it, baby, and grab it on the downslide."

"Well, I missed."

"Noticed," he said, laughing.

Peter caught the disc easily with one hand and immediately turned and threw it to Steve. Kirsten was impressed by the naturally athletic way he moved. Somehow, with his absorption in music, she hadn't expected him to be a good athlete. Terry was impressed, too, when Peter grabbed a speeding throw of his and cast it back with vigorous momentum.

"Geez!" he called. "Cool it, Peter. You're going to take my arm off."

When they were all exhausted, they retreated to the blankets to relax.

What now?" Steve asked.

"Let's just hang out for a few minutes," Rene

answered, pushing her damp hair back from her brow.

"All right to that." Terry leaned back against the tree trunk. "Hand me a soda, will you, Steve? You're closer than I am." He flipped off the top and took a long drink. "Ah, better. So, Steve, I've been meaning to ask you, what are you planning to do with the music next year? Thinking of going the pop route or the classical orchestra way?"

"Not sure. I kind of like both. Maybe I'll mix a little of the two. Then again, it's a matter of what's offered. You've got plans for forming your own group, don't you?"

"I hope to. Long way to go yet. I'll audition for symphonies that have openings, but I really don't think I'd be happy sitting around occupying a chair for years on end. I like to keep moving. Peter's more the guy for single-minded ambition. He really knows where he's headed."

"That so, Peter?" Steve looked interested. "I know you're fantastic on violin. Looking for a first violinist's seat?"

"More," Peter said emphatically. "I'd like to solo—and compose."

Steve lifted his eyebrows. "I'm not on an instrument where I'd think about a solo career, but you're really reaching for the stars. Lots of luck."

"Thanks. I intend to make it if I can."

"What about you, Rene?" Steve inquired. "You've told me you have high hopes, too."

"I really want a first violinist's chair with one of the major orchestras. It may take a few years to work my way up, but I've had my eye on it for a while."

"Of course," Peter put in matter-of-factly, "you're only talking about the time until you get married."

Rene gave him a sharp look. "No, Peter, I'm talking about a lifetime career."

"That's not very realistic, is it?"

"And why not?"

"A professional career demands all your time and energy, and a married woman with a family wouldn't have either."

"Not in my book. My mother owns and manages a dress store, and she's certainly been successful."

"She's an exception. Most women couldn't handle both. Something would suffer. My mother works, too, part-time, but she knows enough to put her family first."

"Peter, I don't get you. Are you living back in the Dark Ages?" Rene asked in disbelief. "Women today have as much right to careers as men. I, for one, don't want to be forced into a role that isn't me."

"It's not a matter of being forced. It's a woman's responsibility."

"What!" Rene glared at him. "You've got to be kidding."

As Kirsten listened, she found it impossible to believe that those words were coming from Peter. It couldn't be the way he felt, not Peter. He'd always been so supportive. Yet now that she thought back, there *had* been a hint or two that he thought her dedication to music was different from his—not so important.

"Peter," she broke in, trying to control her voice, "is this the way you feel about my dreams, too?"

"I respect your dreams, Kirsten. You're extremely talented. You'll do well, but you're a girl, and a girl doesn't have the same drive or incentive as a guy. You'd never have the stamina."

"Wouldn't I? And what of all the years I've put into my music, giving up so much because it was so important to me? That was just fooling around, I suppose."

"No, but eventually you'll lose interest and find your family's more important to you."

"Oh, really? So what you're saying is that a girl can't combine a career and a family."

"Right."

"You said *your* mother works."

100

"She does, but only to help bring in money. My father's job is the important one, and she wouldn't think twice about giving up her job if the family needed her at home. That's how it should be."

"And I'm not normal because I wouldn't be willing to sacrifice everything I've worked for to take a backseat to some guy's ambitions."

"I wouldn't want a girl competing with me every inch of the way."

"No, of course you wouldn't, Peter. Obviously that ego of yours just couldn't take it! How would you feel if someone told you to give up your dreams because there were other things *they* thought were more important?"

"That's not going to happen. I wouldn't be expected to change my career unless I failed at what I was doing."

"But it's OK to expect a girl to forget her dreams, shrug off the years of hard work, waste her talents?"

"You're being ridiculous, Kirsten," Peter said sharply.

By now both Terry and Steve were looking at Peter with amazement.

"*I'm* being ridiculous? You're the one who can't seem to see beyond the nose on your face. All this time when I thought you were supporting me—that we understood each other—you weren't thinking of anyone but Peter Restrochek. The only thing that's important to you is your own success. Who cares about the dreams of a dumb girl!"

"I didn't say you were dumb."

"You might as well have. You've certainly put me down in every other way!" Abruptly she rose. Glaring at Peter, she said, "I'm going back to the dorm."

"Fine! Go!" he yelled, lashing back, his temper boiling. "Go cool off. You're acting like a baby to get angry over such a silly thing."

"Silly? Baby? Oh! Leave me alone!"

As she stormed off, Peter sat scowling, his mouth tight.

Chapter Eleven

That night Kirsten was more confused than she could even admit to herself. It was infuriating that Peter would treat her ambitions so lightly. He'd been so condescending! If that was the way he felt, then good riddance. But she knew another Peter, too, the warm, sympathetic, vulnerable Peter. She missed him. She could barely wait for rehearsal the next day. Maybe he'd give some sign that he was sorry—that the fight would be their first and last.

But the next day Peter didn't make any move to apologize. In fact, he didn't talk to Kirsten at all. She caught him looking at her twice, but he always glanced away as soon as she turned toward him, focusing intently on his music. Of course, she didn't go up and talk to him, either, figuring he ought to make the first move, he ought to apologize to her.

When he continued to ignore her for the rest of the week, Kirsten found herself losing hope of ever resolving her fight with Peter. She was hurt, but it was hard to turn off the feelings that had been growing in her for the last few weeks. As angry as she was, she still cared for him. They'd been so happy together and shared such good times. She tried not to think of all that now, but the memories were so close to the surface. *If only he'd make the tiniest move toward me,* she thought, *I'd be perfectly willing to straighten out this mess we're in.* But he didn't, and Kirsten went through the days feeling more and more hurt and lonely.

About a week after the fight with Peter, Terry came up to Kirsten as she was leaving a music theory class.

"How're you doing?" he asked, stepping close to her and dropping his hand on her shoulder, then he let it slide down her arm.

"Oh, hi, there. I'm fine."

"Are you?" he asked with concern.

"Well," she said, "honestly, I guess I could be better."

"Still upset about that fight with Peter? If it's any consolation, he was out of line."

"I just wish he would admit that."

"He will, give him time. Where are you headed?"

"Back to the dorm, I suppose. Rene and Sharlie usually wait for me, but I don't see them anywhere."

"I'll walk with you. Maybe they went on ahead." Terry stepped even closer to Kirsten, his chest brushing against her shoulder as he took her arm. Kirsten was a little startled at his closeness, and she glanced at him quickly. He smiled firmly and, still holding her arm, steered her across the lawn and toward the dorm. She felt a little strange walking that way with Terry. What if Peter saw? But after a little while, Terry dropped her arm and took a step away from her.

"I sure hope Sharlie's back at the room," he said and smiled.

Kirsten felt a little more comfortable and thought, *I must be getting paranoid. Terry's just trying to cheer me up.* "You two have been getting along real well together."

"I like to think so," he said, grinning.

"She's not nearly so shy as she was in the beginning of the summer."

Terry laughed. "Leave someone around me long enough, and they're bound to lose their shyness."

"It didn't seem to work with Peter."

"No, I suppose you're the one working the miracles there."

"I *was*," Kirsten said with emphasis.

"Listen, chin up. All's not lost."

Kirsten smiled a little wryly.

The next day at lunch Kirsten sensed someone sit down next to her on the lawn. She turned, hoping it was Peter, and found Terry beside her.

"Mind if I sit with you?" he said.

"Please do. Sharlie and Rene are late."

"I saw them talking to Mr. Caldfrey. They should be out in a minute." Terry looked up. Kirsten followed his gaze and saw Peter staring across the lawn at them. *He looks pretty angry,* she thought. *He's absolutely red in the face. He must really hate me.*

"It sounds better and better every day—the orchestra, I mean," Terry continued, breaking into her thoughts.

"Yes. It does," Kirsten answered mechanically. She was so intent on Peter that she barely heard Terry. She was completely taken aback when Terry picked up her hand and held it casually as Peter passed. "Oh, hi, Peter," he said nonchalantly.

Peter grunted a greeting and frowned at his

friend. Kirsten dropped her gaze so she wouldn't have to see his scowl. *What's going on?* she thought, quickly breaking Terry's grasp.

"Sorry, I shouldn't have done that," he said, and he gave her that same firm smile he'd given her the other day when he'd taken her arm. He looked down at his sandwich, then said, "You know, Peter's been like a zombie lately. I can tell he's feeling pretty low. He's not even concentrating on his music."

"Really? Has he said anything to you?" Funny, a moment before Terry had been flirting with her, but now he just seemed worried about his friends—both Peter and her.

"No, I've tried to bring it up, but he changes the subject."

"Let's face it, Terry. I think he's just changed his mind about me."

"No, I don't think so. Give him a little more time, Kirsten. He didn't mean to be nasty the other day. He's had it rough—no money. And his family just doesn't appreciate his talents. I met them once when I went with him to pick up some things he'd left at home. Nice people, but with really old-fashioned values. When Peter was out of the room, the first thing his father said to me was, 'What does he want with all this music? It's not going to get him a job.' I told him that it could get Peter a great job with a symphony orchestra. He just said, 'I'm talking about the real world—a trade so he can support a family. He's dreaming.'

"I know what he said about your career upset you, but those are the only kind of values he could ever have gotten from his family. He's hurting right now, and I think he needs to do some serious thinking. He's stubborn, and it'll take him a while before he realizes and admits how wrong he was. I could try to talk to him, but I don't think it would do much good. He's got to figure it out for himself."

"I've been trying to give him the benefit of the doubt, but it's so hard, Terry. He'll hardly look at me."

"I know, I'd be feeling pretty rotten if something like this had happened to Sharlie and me."

"I know you're trying to make me feel better," Kirsten said, attempting to smile, "and I appreciate it."

"No problem, anything I can do."

The summer that had started out so wonderfully for Kirsten was falling apart. Rene and Sharlie were still as friendly as ever, but they weren't around too much. They did a lot of things without her now—just the two of them—and Kirsten felt really left out. Peter didn't talk to her or even look at her. She did still see a lot of Terry, but at times she felt uncomfortable with him. She was sure he wasn't interested in her as a girlfriend, but once in a while he'd stand too close to her or stroke her hair. He never did it when they were alone. She couldn't figure it out; but it did annoy her because she knew Peter had seen them a few times. What could he think?

One day after rehearsal while they were standing on the lawn Kirsten asked Rene if she wanted to walk into town. She shook her head and said, "Sorry, Sharlie and I have some errands to do."

She didn't even ask me to come, thought Kirsten, close to tears. But she just said, "Oh, well, I guess I'll go do some practicing instead."

As they were talking, Terry had come up to them. "I'll walk over to the practice sheds with you, Kirsten. I've got to go over some music."

"Sure, Terry," said Kirsten, turning down the path. She looked up and saw Peter. He was just standing and glaring at them. Terry took her arm and, as he had the first time, steered her down the path.

Peter stiffened when he saw them approaching.

"Hi, Peter, how's everything?" said Terry.

"Where are you going?" asked Peter as if it

were a challenge. He stared angrily at Terry, obviously avoiding Kirsten's eyes.

"We're just going to practice a little," Terry said as if nothing were wrong. *Oh no*, thought Kirsten, *Peter's going to think Terry and I are going to practice together. That used to be Peter's thing to do with me.*

Peter didn't say a word as he turned and walked away.

"Terry," Kirsten said angrily, pulling away from him so quickly she nearly dropped the music she was carrying, "why don't you stay away from me when Peter's around? Can't you see what it looks like to him? Can't you see how angry he's getting?" She ran down the path away from Terry so he wouldn't see her starting to cry.

"Wait, Kirsten," he yelled, "you don't understand. . . ."

Kirsten walked and walked until her tears stopped. Then she headed back to the dorm; she didn't feel like practicing. *Rene and Sharlie are probably still doing their stupid chores*, she thought. *Some good friends they turned out to be. They've practically deserted me when I need them the most. And Terry's probably ruined any chance I had with Peter.*

She trudged unhappily toward the dorm. A number of kids were sitting on lawn chairs outside. Not wanting anyone to stop her, she quickened her pace and headed determinedly for the front door. Out of the corner of her eye, she spotted Rene, sitting to the right of the door. Realizing that she couldn't ignore her, Kirsten turned. There sat Rene, Sharlie, *and* Terry, all staring at her with guilty expressions on their faces. Kirsten looked at her friends in confusion. Why were they looking at her like that? What had they been talking about? It almost seemed as though they'd planned this little get-together when they knew she'd be away. No one even said hello to her.

She grasped her music to her chest. "Uh—I guess I'm interrupting something. You guys go ahead—I've got some stuff to do."

Barely concealing the tears in her eyes, she raced inside the dorm. She had just reached the foot of the stairs when she heard someone running after her.

"Kirsten, wait! Please, come back. There's something we want to explain to you."

"It's all right, Rene."

"No, it's not all right."

"I didn't mean to interrupt anything."

"Maybe it's better you did. We've been playing a little trick on you—with all good intentions—but I think it's time we let you in on it."

"I don't understand. What trick?"

Rene sighed. "You'll understand in a minute."

Totally bewildered, Kirsten let Rene lead her back outside to where Terry and Sharlie were sitting. They looked up sheepishly.

"I told Kirsten we had something to tell her," Rene said quickly. "I think she deserves to know what's going on."

"I couldn't agree more," Terry said. "I was afraid all along this little scheme would backfire."

"Sit down," said Rene, pulling up another lawn chair. "Before I begin to explain, I just want you to know we all meant the best—for both you and Peter."

Kirsten's heart sank. What had they been up to? Had they done something that had ruined her chances with Peter forever?

"We were all upset about your fight," Rene went on briskly, sitting down. "And seeing the two of you moping around, both too proud and stubborn to do anything about making up—we decided to try and help things along. It was my idea actually. I talked the other two into it, so if you're angry, you can blame me."

"We're just as much at fault," Terry interrupted. "No one made us go along with it, and I certainly played the biggest part."

"Well, that's beside the point now." Rene took a deep breath and continued. "We knew you both still cared about each other, but you weren't ever going to straighten things out unless you started talking again. Since neither of you would break down and make the first move, I figured maybe we could make Peter jealous, so jealous he'd forget his pride."

"So she volunteered me for the job," said Terry. "I was pretty skeptical at first. I didn't want either you or Peter to get hurt any worse. And I was worried that our little game might ruin my friendship with Peter forever. But I decided that if I was *really* a good friend, I'd try to help Peter—help you, too, even if I came off looking pretty rotten—I mean, making a play for my best friend's girlfriend right in front of him. Then when I saw how upset you were today, I ran over here to talk about it."

Kirsten listened, inwardly cringing when she thought of how easily she'd been duped, how she hadn't seen through Terry's sudden interest in her. But, in spite of everything, she wasn't angry with any of them; they had meant well. She was upset, of course, but not angry.

But Peter, what must he think of her to latch on to Terry so quickly when only a week before she had been in love with him?

"What about you and Sharlie?" she asked in a weak voice.

"I knew it was all for a greater cause," Sharlie replied, smiling. "Besides, it wasn't as if Terry was making a *real* play for you. We figured you might not even notice because you were so busy moping about Peter."

"So that's why I started paying so much attention to you, especially at rehearsals and lunch, where I knew Peter would see us. And, wow, did he see us."

"Is that the reason you two were always running off together?" Kirsten asked Rene and Sharlie. "To leave me alone with Terry?"

"That's right."

"Boy, I was beginning to think you hated me, too!" she said with a sad smile.

"What do you mean 'too'?" asked Terry. "If you're talking about Peter, he doesn't hate you. It's me he sees as the villain."

"Oh?"

"He's never said a word against you, only agreed with all the good things I said about you. It's me he's mad at." He frowned. "With good reason. He's so jealous, Kirsten, I can't believe he hasn't punched me out."

Kirsten shook her head. Knowing Peter as well as she did, she knew that the competition from Terry might just push him back into his shell. He wasn't secure enough yet to be aggressive about a relationship.

"So, that's it," Rene finished. "We're really

sorry, Kirsten. I can see by your face you're upset."

"I guess I am upset. I had no idea."

"If it weren't for me and my harebrained scheme!" Rene threw up her hands. "I'm really a jerk."

"You didn't mean to get me upset. But I'm glad you told me because I know this is much more than Peter can handle."

"Listen, if you think it would help," Terry suggested, "I'll go tell Peter everything."

Kirsten shook her head. "He'd really feel self-conscious if he thought you were making a fool of him."

"You're right. We didn't think of the total effect this would have on Peter; we just weren't thinking, I guess. Anyway, now that I won't be pretending to make a play for you anymore, maybe it will all blow over."

Terry, Rene, and Sharlie all looked miserable, and Kirsten knew she'd have to fix things up with Peter or they'd all have a really rotten time for the rest of the summer.

Chapter Twelve

Terry didn't know, as he headed back to the dorm later that afternoon, that the episode was far from over; Peter's patience had finally run out. Peter was pacing their room, thinking about the scene he'd watched that afternoon as Terry had taken Kirsten's arm. He'd had enough of watching his friend with Kirsten.

Terry entered the room, took one look at Peter's face and clenched fists, and knew Peter had had it. He hadn't taken three steps into the room when Peter's voice stopped him.

"I want to talk to you."

Terry heard the fury in his friend's voice. He didn't know whether to quickly try and explain what he had been trying to do or to hear Peter

116

out. He decided to let Peter talk first. Terry tried to sound casual as he said, "Sure. What's on your mind?"

"I want to know what's going on." Peter moved to within inches of Terry, standing tall and staring down at him. "I've had it with you hanging all over Kirsten! Don't you care about my feelings? You knew what Kirsten and I had going together. The first time in my life I ever cared about a girl! You had to know what was going on, but what do you do? You move in the first second I'm out of the picture. Yeah, we had a fight, but we could have patched it up—I *know* we could have! You and I have been good friends, but not anymore. I want to know what's going on."

"Peter, Peter." Terry put up his hands in defense. "Cool it, will you? Let me explain!"

"Explain what? I've seen the two of you."

"There's something I have to explain."

"More than *one* thing you have to explain!"

"Listen! Will you *please* listen. Unclench your fists! You'd probably knock me out if you ever hit me, you're so mad."

"I'm listening, Terry," he said through his teeth.

Terry swallowed. "OK. Look, we've been pulling a fast one on you—me, Rene, and Sharlie. We thought—and I know it was stupid now—

but we thought that maybe if I made you jealous enough, you'd try to get back together with Kirsten. We thought *we* could do something to help. All right, it was really a dumb idea."

Terry drew a deep breath, noticing that Peter looked as if he weren't quite following what Terry was saying. "The plan was for me to make a play for Kirsten so you would get jealous and try to get her back. Of course, I didn't *really* make a play for her. Most of the time when you saw us, we were talking about how rotten she was feeling. Don't worry, she never thought I was making a play. She was thinking about you too much to really pay attention to what I was doing. And we told her everything this afternoon—Rene, Sharlie, and I. She wasn't too happy about it. Neither am I, now that it's all done. It was a rotten trick to pull on you. We should have just let you fix it up yourselves."

Peter glared at Terry. "What I don't understand, is how you could trick me like this! I must look like such an idiot."

"I'm sorry, Peter."

"Did you think I was such a wimp I couldn't get Kirsten back by myself?"

"We were wrong, but we were only trying to help."

Peter didn't seem to hear him. "I've been worrying myself sick, and it was all a game!"

"Well, if we thought you were doing *one* thing to get Kirsten back, we wouldn't have interfered, but what did you do?"

"All right, nothing. But I was going to."

"When?"

"I had to think it through."

"And somehow make your behavior at the picnic that day seem all right?"

"Well, I was right. It's just that I came on a little strong."

"Do you really think that, Peter?"

"Why not?"

"Because you're wrong. Kirsten and the other girls have worked for what they've got, just like we did. You made it sound like it was terrible for them to want careers. I know your background and where you're coming from, but, Peter, this time you're just wrong. You want to escape from the life you knew as a kid—well, you may have, but your opinions and ideas about women are stuck back in Newark. You're a pro with music but you don't understand people." As soon as the words were out of his mouth, Terry realized he was coming on too strong. "I've said too much."

"So you're telling me I'm an idiot?"

"No, just that you were wrong about what you said to Kirsten. Peter, you must know she's got a lot of talent, a lot of pride, just like you.

What's more important is that she's a terrific girl, and you hurt her."

"I just told her and Rene what I thought."

"Would you like to have your words repeated back to you? Think about it, Peter. Really think. I can't believe you're that narrow-minded, but I can't put thoughts in your head, you've got to think it through for yourself. She cares about you and likes you for what you are and what you've done. She expects you to like her for what *she* is and what *she's* done. You can't, though, can you?" He paused. "So what are you going to do?"

"I don't know."

"Swallow your pride, Peter. You know you're hurting her!"

"She's hurting me."

"She only hurt you because you came down on what she believed in. You said rotten things."

Peter's anger was turning to doubt. "You sure there's not more to the way she's been acting than that? Maybe she's using our argument as an excuse to break up with me."

"No way. Look, I know you don't have much experience with girls, but I do. I've seen the way Kirsten's acting, and I've talked to her. She was upset and angry at first, and now she's just sad. But she won't come to you, and I think she's perfectly right in expecting you to apologize."

Peter was staring out the window, deep in thought. Finally he sighed. "I've been trying to figure out how to go to her, what to say—whether I even should try. When I saw you two together, I just thought she didn't care anymore. I didn't know what to do, except to get angrier and angrier."

"We were wrong," Terry admitted. "Well, what are you going to do?"

"I don't know. I need to let this sink in."

"No hard feelings?"

"No."

"Then let's shake on it." Terry offered his hand. "And if there's anything I can do, just ask—but no more interfering, I promise."

Peter took his friend's hand, returning the firm clasp. "I'm glad you told me this—I just wish you'd told me sooner."

"So do I. It would've avoided a lot of misunderstandings." Terry checked his watch. "I've got to meet with the quartet. I can skip it if you want to talk some more."

"No, go on. I'm going to take a walk and decide what to do."

"I won't tell Kirsten that I talked to you."

"Please don't. It's between her and me now."

Chapter Thirteen

Sharlie was late for dinner that night, and Rene and Kirsten took a table in a corner where they could talk privately. Kirsten had no appetite and pushed the food around her plate as Rene sat somber faced, very unlike her usual self.

"I wish there was something I could do to patch things up for you," she mused. "I feel pretty responsible for this mess."

"Please, Rene. I told you not to blame yourself. You meant well."

Rene took a sip of her soda. "Have you decided what you're going to do?"

"No. I'm debating. If he doesn't say anything to me by tomorrow after rehearsal, I'll go talk to him. I have to clear the air. I just wish I knew what was going through his head."

"Terry thinks he's really sorry and misses you."

"I know, but after what's happened the past few days—" Kirsten shrugged. "And if we do get back together, it's got to be because he likes me for what I am and what I want to be and doesn't expect me to pretend to be someone I'm not."

Just then Sharlie came rushing across the room. Her cheeks were flushed with excitement.

"Well," Rene looked up. "Where have you been? You were supposed to meet us here half an hour ago."

"I ran into Terry on my way here. Boy, do I have news for you!"

"Oh?" said Kirsten and Rene simultaneously.

"Yeah. Just let me get my dinner before they put all the food away. I'm starved."

"At a moment like this you're thinking of food?"

"I'll only be a sec."

"I wonder what her news is? It must be good, or she wouldn't be so excited." Kirsten sounded happier than she had in days.

"We'll find out in a minute."

Sharlie came back with her tray and slid into the empty chair. "OK, here it is. I didn't get to talk too long to Terry, but I think I've got the important details. When he got back to his room this afternoon, Peter was waiting for him, and, boy, was he mad! Terry thought he was going to haul off and punch him. Peter had noticed all the attention Terry was paying Kirsten, and he wanted to know what Terry had on his mind. Well, Terry didn't have much choice at that point but to tell Peter what we'd been up to and that the whole thing was a plan to get Peter jealous. Oh, don't worry, Kirsten, Terry told Peter very clearly that you had nothing to do with it.

"The long and the short of it is that they finally talked over the way Peter had acted that day. Peter was stubborn, but Terry thinks he's finally begun to see the light. He just didn't realize how close minded he's been or how badly he hurt you. All he could think about was that you'd hurt him." She paused and bit into a roll.

"And?"

"Terry doesn't know. When he finally left for his quartet rehearsal, Peter only said that he was going for a walk—he had some thinking to do. But he and Terry shook hands, and Peter said there were no hard feelings."

"Did he say he was going to talk to Kirsten?"

"He didn't say what he was going to do."

Kirsten, who had silently been letting this news sink in, spoke quietly. "So now he knows why I was so angry, and if he doesn't come and talk to me tomorrow, I'll have to figure it's finished between us." She sighed. "But he *was* jealous?"

"You can bet on that. He was livid. Terry said that for a guy to get that jealous has to be a sign he really cares."

"But now his pride's involved again. He'll be too embarrassed to make the first move. He probably thinks he looked like a fool."

"At first. But Terry told him that the *last* thing we wanted was to make him feel bad. He was acting like a jerk by not talking to you, not by getting jealous."

"He still may be afraid to talk to me."

"Well," said Rene practically, "you'd already decided that if he didn't come to you tomorrow, you'd go talk to him."

"But things are different now. I'm embarrassed, too. I suppose I *will* talk to him, though, if only to find out where I stand. Oh," she shook her head and let out a long sigh. "Maybe I was better off without a boyfriend. I had no idea things could get so complicated."

"Don't worry," put in Sharlie. "It's going to work out, and think of all the excitement you'd be missing. I sure wouldn't give up this summer even if something went wrong between Terry and me. For the first time in my life I feel like someone except 'shy Sharlie.' "

"You're right," Kirsten said and slowly nodded her head. "I wouldn't want to give it up, either. Keep your fingers crossed for me."

"We will."

As the girls left the dining room a half hour later, Kirsten was surprised to see Mrs. Vertel motioning to her from the hallway.

"Can you come here a moment, Kirsten? I have something for you."

"Sure. Be right there." She turned to Rene and Sharlie. "Go on. I'll be up in a minute."

When Mrs. Vertel handed her the long, white envelope, Kirsten at first thought it was a letter from her parents. Then she flipped it over and saw the handwriting. Peter's. She was sure it was Peter's. Her stomach immediately started to flutter, but she tried not to let it.

"A nice young man dropped it off while you were at dinner," Mrs. Vertel was saying. "I told him he could go in and deliver it in person, but he said no."

Already Kirsten's mind was reeling. What did Peter have to say that he couldn't say in person? That he had to say in a letter? If it *was* a letter. *Maybe he's returning all the music I wrote him,* she thought. She barely heard Mrs. Vertel's good night as she turned toward the stairs, her heart pounding.

Kirsten walked to her room in a daze, torn

between anticipation and fear of what she'd find. Rene and Sharlie couldn't miss her worried expression as she walked into the room.

"What's wrong?" Sharlie was the first to speak. "You look as though you've seen a ghost."

"Not bad news, I hope!" Rene added.

"I don't know." Kirsten's voice trembled. "It's a letter from Peter."

"Oh!" Both girls stared.

"Listen," Sharlie said quickly. "You probably want to be alone. Rene and I can go out for a walk."

Before Kirsten could say a word, the two girls were at the door. "We'll be back in an hour or so if you want to talk."

Kirsten nodded. If the envelope contained bad news, she knew she wouldn't be able to stop crying, and she didn't want her friends to see that. Sitting down on her bed, she made a silent wish before opening the envelope that she'd like what was inside. Then she ran her thumb under the flap.

Her eyes fastened first on the five sheets of music that fell into her lap. With it was a letter. Her fingers trembled as she picked it up and slowly unfolded it.

Chapter Fourteen

At half-past three the next afternoon Kirsten sat nervously in the rehearsal room. Spread out before her on the piano were five sheets of handwritten music. She repositioned them, checked her watch, and adjusted the folding screen that divided the shed into two small working areas. Everything was ready. As she sat down again on the piano bench, she tried to relax. If only her plan would work.

From the pocket of her jeans, she pulled out the much read and folded letter that Peter had sent her the night before. She let her eyes skim over the words, although she had them memorized by now.

Kirsten,

Ever since the day of the picnic, I've wanted to talk to you but didn't know how to do it or what to say. I've done a lot of thinking since then. I realize what a great person you are. I was wrong. I wouldn't have done anything to hurt you deliberately, but by now I know you must be totally fed up with me. I can understand that, and I don't blame you. I'm not very good at putting things into words as you know, so I've written this song for you to try to tell you how wonderful it's been to know you and that I won't forget you. I hope you're not too angry to play it just once.

Peter

Kirsten heard the sounds of voices and footsteps. Quickly she refolded the letter and stuffed it back into her pocket. She lifted her fingers to the keyboard. She desperately hoped Terry had been able to arrange things the way she'd asked him. There was a creak and then the sound of the door opening. With the screen in place, she and the piano were hidden from anyone entering through the doorway. She heard voices at the other side of the room, one bright, the other dejected.

That was her cue. Immediately she brought her fingers to the keys and launched into the music.

There was sudden silence from the other side of the room. She was sorry that the screen that hid her from view also prevented her from seeing what was going on.

She forced herself to relax and continue playing with as much feeling as possible.

She heard a startled exclamation. "What is this?"

"Just listen."

She heard footsteps, and then the door opened and closed. Only one person had left, though, because she heard someone breathing in the room. She played on. Again she heard footsteps, this time moving toward the screen. Her heart was in her throat. What if it didn't work the way she wanted?

In a moment she looked up from the music and saw Peter standing beside the screen, staring at her. She tried to smile, but her lips trembled. This was the last section of the song, the most important part, and it had to be perfect. She put all her soul into it, the feeling she was drawing from the written notes intensifying as she saw the happiness in Peter's eyes, the beginning of a smile on his lips.

They watched each other as the last chords of his composition filled the air.

Then the song was finished. She brought her now-shaking hands down to her lap. He was striding toward her, around the piano, reaching down.

"Kirsten—oh, Kirsten." His voice was anxious. "Does this mean what I think—hope—it means?"

"Yes. Peter, I couldn't let you end it like that—ending it was what you meant in your note, wasn't it?"

"I never thought you'd forgive me for being such a blockhead. I know, Terry told me you cared, and I wanted to believe it, but you're so pretty, so talented, so nice—why would you want to keep wasting your time with a mixed-up musician like me? A kid from the poor side of Newark who's got his ideals so confused, he doesn't know a good thing when it's staring him in the face."

"You're being too hard on yourself. Besides, it doesn't matter to me where you come from. I care about you for what *you* are."

He seemed almost afraid to believe her. "I'm not going to try to blame the way I acted on anyone else. But the way I was brought up, I just never thought of women having great ambitions. My mother and my sisters worked hard, but at menial stuff, and only to make

131

ends meet. They never loved what they were doing. My mother always used to say that her family and home were her first priority, and that was the way it should be. The man was the breadwinner."

He took a deep breath and continued as though he had a lot to say. "I didn't mean to put you down, Kirsten, and the more I thought about it, the more I understood that what I liked about you from the beginning was that you were smart and talented and cared enough about music to give up other things so that someday you would be one of the best. You looked at a career in music just the way I looked at it myself. I don't know why I thought that was OK for me but not for you."

"Stop, Peter." She reached up and touched her hand to his lips. "You've said all I've been waiting to hear. I can understand how hard it must have been for you to understand all this. When you've been brought up thinking one way, it isn't easy to turn around and look at things just the opposite." She smiled. "I guess what's most important to me is that you cared enough about me to try."

"Do—do you mean then," he asked breathlessly, "that you're willing to forgive me—to start over?"

She nodded.

"I'd like that, Kirsten."

"So would I."

He gently pulled her up to stand facing him and for a moment hugged her close. "Oh, Kirsten!" Then he leaned back so he could look down at her face. "I promise never to put you down again. I see things so much differently now than I did a few weeks ago."

"I know, and I've learned a lot, too—learned how nice it is to be with a person who understands me and likes the same things I do."

"It doesn't have to end this summer. I mean, I don't want it to. We talked about you coming down to Trilling—" He paused.

Kirsten laughed. "Do you think I would have said all I've just said if I expected it to end this summer?"

He grinned crookedly. "I *am* a blockhead, aren't I? Kirsten, you're the best." His eyes grew soft as he pulled her close again, letting his arms circle her so that she was pressed tightly against his chest.

"Mmm." Kirsten sighed into Peter's shoulder.

He rubbed his cheek against her hair. "There are so many other things I feel I should be telling you."

"We have time."

"That's a nice thought."

She lifted her head from his chest. Slowly he

rubbed his finger down the side of her face, then he lowered his head and brought his lips gently to hers. It was a kiss that sent her heart flying—a beautiful start to their new beginning.

*Here's a preview
of a fabulous new series from the
publisher of Sweet Dreams,®
coming to your bookshops very soon.*

SWEET VALLEY HIGH™

Step inside the halls of Sweet Valley High, and meet the stars of Bantam's new series—sixteen-year-old twin sisters Elizabeth and Jessica Wakefield. Physically the girls are identical. Both have the same sun-streaked, shoulder-length blonde hair, green-blue eyes, cameo skin, and radiant smiles. Both are five feet six on the button and wear the same size dress, jeans and shoes. But there the similarity ends.

Jessica Wakefield is captain of the cheering squad, a great dancer, very popular with boys, sparkling, coquettish, adorable, and about as devious, conniving, and selfish as any sixteen-year-old could possibly be.

Elizabeth is her mirror image. While Jessica is a performer, Liz is the poet. In fact, she would like to be a writer. Unknown to anyone, except Mr. Collins, the faculty adviser of the high school newspaper, Liz writes the "Eyes and Ears" column, which everyone reads for the latest gossip scoops. Her column is bright and funny and on the mark but never cruel. That's the way Liz is. She cares about other people. She's open, honest, loyal, generous, and considerate. She's the best friend you'll ever have. You can lean on her, trust her to come through when you need her, and enjoy her because, along with all her other attributes, she sparkles. She's fun.

Jessica Wakefield is another sort altogether. She takes shameless advantage of her sister. And, for the most part, Elizabeth lets her. When it comes to her twin, Liz is a soft touch. Not a complete pushover, but easier than she should be.

Jessica always knows how to get to her sister. She starts with the simple premise that Liz believes the best about people, in particular her twin. Jessica is not above using her sister's identity when it comes in handy or, for that matter, her boyfriend. She's very possessive of Liz and resents anyone, boy or girl, getting too close. Watch out if you're planning to be Liz's friend. Poor Enid Rollins.

Enid is Liz's best friend. She's quiet and smart; pretty, too, though you might not even notice her until she smiles her dazzling smile. But beneath the smile is the terrible secret of Enid's past, a secret she desperately wants to keep buried from her new boyfriend, Ronnie Edwards, and especially from the likes of Jessica and her scheming friend Lila.

Lila Fowler is the richest girl in all of Sweet Valley. While the Wakefields live in the valley's comfortable development, Lila lives with her father in a fabulous mansion "on the hill." She has her own car, an endless allowance, a string of credit cards, and no curfew. Glamorous, stylish, and almost as devious as Jessica, she's the only girl in Sweet Valley who can occasionally beat Jessica at her own game. If Jessica's a 10 on the schemer scale, Lila's a solid 8.

While Lila Fowler is the richest girl in town, Bruce Patman is the richest boy. Outrageously attractive, with dark hair and big blue eyes, he's also a fabulous tennis player. The black Porsche he drives doesn't hurt his image either. But Bruce is a super-spoiled snob. Jessica really meets her match in him. They seem destined for each other ...

If Jessica and Bruce's love match is stormy, Liz's romance with basketball star Todd Wilkins is purest sunshine. His lean, tall good looks attract Liz from the first. And Todd seems to feel the same way. But when Jessica's greedy gaze falls on Todd, she's smart enough to size him up as a good thing, too. And she's certainly unscrupulous enough to go for it.

Does it sound like Sweet Valley High is a hotbed of social intrigue? Well, it is. And one of the people who tries to keep the lid on is good-hearted Mr. Collins. A tall, slim strawberry blonde in tweed jackets and corduroys, Mr. Collins is faculty advisor to the high school newspaper and a special friend of Elizabeth's. Jessica's head over heels about him, too.

Where is all this drama taking place? In the town of Sweet Valley, located in a gorgeous corner of sunswept Southern California. The town is small and charming, though the peace is getting harder to keep, as old money (the Patman clan) wars with new (Lila Fowler's father). Sweet Valley has a pharmacy, a tiny movie house, a couple of gift shops, and a pizza place on Main Street. Around the corner are the library and a tiny grocery store. But most of the action is at the mall, a shopping center located five miles from town. There you'll find all you need for a day's entertainment: lots of stores, a video arcade, two twin movie theaters, and a giant supermarket.

It's only fifteen minutes to the beach from Sweet Valley. Kids often head out there after school, stopping on the way at the Dairi Burger for fried clams and a shake. Some of them bypass the Dairi Burger for a dingy roadhouse just across the highway. Inside, the bar is dark and dirty, and the songs on the jukebox are hopelessly out of date. But that's where the fast crowd goes, and often the college kids. Who said they saw Elizabeth Wakefield there in Book One of SWEET VALLEY HIGH? Find out in ...

DOUBLE LOVE

coming early in the New Year, the
first in this exciting new series
from the publishers of Sweet Dreams.

If you would like to know more about Sweet Valley High, or have difficulty obtaining the books locally, or if you would like to tell us what you think of the series, write to:-

Kim Prior, Corgi Books, Century House, 61–63 Uxbridge Road, London W5 5SA,

or

Sally Porter, Corgi/Bantam Books, 26 Harley Crescent, Condell Park, Sydney, NSW 2200, AUSTRALIA.